MW00650494

CLOCKWORK SAMURAI

BOOK 2: THE GUNPOWDER CHRONICLES

JEANNIE LIN

CLOCKWORK SAMURAI
Print: ISBN: 978-0-9909462-5-0

Copyright © 2015 by Jeannie Lin
Cover design © Deranged Doctor Design (www.derangeddoctordesign.com)

Publishing History

First edition: InterMix eBook Edition / November 2015

Second edition: Jeannie Lin Edition / October 2017

All rights reserved. This book or any portion thereof may not be reproduced, distributed or used in any form or manner without the express written permission of the publisher except for the use of brief quotations in a book review.

For inquiries, contact Jeannie Lin using the e-mail contact form at:
www.jeannielin.com

❀ Created with Vellum

1

Qing Dynasty, 1852 A.D.

One might think that it was difficult for a woman to become a physician, and even more difficult to rise in the ranks of the imperial palace. But both assumptions are untrue.

Women have ailments and concerns that are particular to the female sex—there is no denying that. And every emperor since the First Dynasty has kept a harem of wives and consorts and concubines that had to remain in good health. And as no grown man, other than the Emperor, could be allowed near his precious imperial women, harem physicians were traditionally eunuchs or women themselves. It was for this reason that I had been appointed to the Court of Physicians, deep within the Forbidden City. I had considered it a great, great honor at the time.

Each morning, I would arrive at the apothecary before dawn to light the medicine stoves. Then I would get to work.

Today I was scheduled to visit the harem. I had a book containing the names of the imperial concubines and all the various medicines they were required to take. With the book in hand, I headed toward the storage room.

There must have been a thousand remedies stored in the cavernous chamber. The rosewood cabinets stretched from floor to ceiling, with rows upon rows of meticulously labeled drawers. Inside, one could find every herb or plant known to man. A cure for every ailment and disease, from ginger root for stomach pains to elixirs containing ground pearl and quicksilver rumored to grant immortality.

There were even medicines imported from the West that I had only recently begun to study. The other physicians regarded the bottles with a wary eye. I tended to agree. Who knew what had been mixed into those strange liquids?

I set the book down, page open to the first set of ingredients, and placed a porcelain bowl beneath the dispensing basin. A series of winding tubes snaked out from the cabinets leading into the receptacle. At the base of each of the cabinets was a set of brass dials.

All I had to do was turn the dials to indicate which ingredients I needed. Once the correct symbols were aligned, I pulled a lever and the cabinets whirred to life as the gears inside engaged. The drawers shifted open and closed, releasing the desired amount of each herb down the delivery tubes. By now, I knew the combinations by heart. My hands flew over the dials, aligning the symbols with a satisfying click and pulling the lever. After the first set, I replaced the bowl and started on the next set of herbs. Longan berries, ginseng, angelica.

I gave each bowl one last check before carrying them back to the stoves. Then I poured the contents into separate brewing pots to steep.

Each formula had been prescribed by the head physician to warm the blood and awaken the internal organs. And most important of all, to increase fertility. Yizhu had been Emperor for over a year now, having taken the throne before I was appointed to the physicians' court.

The empire did need an heir, but to my knowledge women

became pregnant fairly well without the aid of special teas and treatments. This was part of the ritual of the palace. The Forbidden City was ruled by ritual.

As fast as I tried to work, it always took me hours before the process was complete. The sun was high by the time I started ladling the mixtures into serving bowls. I had nearly finished when a messenger was announced.

The dragon insignia on the servant's robe sent the maidservants scurrying aside. This was a messenger from the Inner Court.

"The Emperor summons Physician Jin Soling to the Palace of Heavenly Purity," he announced.

I was still standing with ladle in one hand, empty bowl in the other, and barely time to wipe my brow. The heat from the stoves had turned the chamber into an oven.

Even as unpresentable as I was, there was no questioning an imperial order. I gave a few brief instructions to the attending eunuchs, then followed immediately behind the messenger as he made his way through the courtyards and corridors toward the heart of the Forbidden City.

I hadn't spoken to Yizhu since he took the throne. Despite residing in the palace, I'd barely seen him. By tradition, Yizhu was still in mourning for his late father, and I couldn't imagine why he'd want to speak to me now.

A great cage of steel encased the palaces and halls of the Inner Court where the Emperor and his Grand Council held court. The sight of the dome made my blood run cold. To me, it looked as if the Inner Court had been imprisoned.

The fortifications had been put in place after the empire's defeat against the *Yangguizi*. The dome, with its black metal bars, ran counter to a thousand years of palace architecture. There was no elegance or beauty to it. Along with the dome, imperial builders had erected watchtowers and cannon fortifications around the city. The imperial air fleet had tripled in size. Though our treaty with the *Yangguizi* restricted them to the trading ports, the Grand Council knew an airship fleet could reach Peking within days.

I stepped beneath the dome where a spider web shadow blocked out the sun, allowing it only to filter in through tiny lines and squares. Immediately the air felt heavier. When we reached the main courtyard of the inner palace, the feeling of dread only worsened.

The triple halls of the Inner Court had been with built with an eye for beauty and harmony, but that was all ruined now. The steel cage had come down to block out the heavens. It had been installed with a heavy hand, without any sense of balance. It told us danger was everywhere. The invasion was already upon us.

The Palace of Heavenly Purity rose from a white marble foundation, as if floating above the clouds. The messenger stood aside as I climbed the steps toward a set of brass studded doors. They swung open as I approached, pulled by an invisible hand.

Inside, my heart pounded as I passed beneath the watchful eye of the palace guards. The only thing that moved was their eyes as they tracked my every footstep.

The breath rushed out of me when I saw the throne at the end of the cavernous audience hall. Emperor Yizhu sat upon the carved seat, which was gilded with gold leaf and framed on either side by a red columns. Each column was inscribed, but I had little time to read the words. Yizhu was staring down at me from behind his desk—the desk from which he determined the fate of the land.

I bowed and lowered my gaze before moving forward. My father had been summoned like this. He'd made this very same long walk on his last night on this earth.

At the foot of the dais, I started to kneel but was met with an impatient huff.

"Come," Yizhu spat out. "The Emperor has no time to wait."

My eyes flickered upward. Even though it was a direct order, I remained frozen. I had known Yizhu before he was emperor, but even then he'd frightened me.

"Well?" he challenged.

Though he sounded cross, the last part held a hint of informality. I set one foot upon the dais, and then another. An attendant came forward to set a tray upon the desk before retreating. I was left alone on the platform with the Son of Heaven.

Yizhu was dressed in an imperial yellow robe embroidered with a dragon, the eternal symbol of the Emperor, but the material seemed to hang heavily upon his shoulders. There was a gauntness about his face as he scowled at me with his eyebrows stabbing sharply downward.

A year had done much to transform him. Not long ago, he'd been a haughty young prince with grand ideas. Now he was a too-young emperor with a troubled empire.

At twenty, he was only a year older than me, but he seemed much older. Not in his face, which had a decidedly youthful look, or his hair, which was jet-black and braided into a thick queue in the Manchurian style. It was in his eyes.

Those eyes spoke of sleepless nights. The shadows beneath them were deep and haunted.

"Closer." He waved me up the final step and gestured toward the tray. "I have two armies battling in my head. Neither one will surrender."

Yizhu squeezed his eyes shut and rubbed a hand over his temple. I finally saw what the attendant had set down before him. The tray was lined with a set of long silver needles.

"They say you can work wonders, Physician Jin. Rid me of this headache."

His eyes remained closed as I scanned the instruments. Certainly they had been tested for any poisonous substances. Even so, I was nervous about laying my hands on our sovereign. What if I made some grave mistake?

"Are you suddenly afraid of me, Jin Soling?"

Yizhu's eyes slitted open as he taunted me. He had the characteristic broad forehead and sharp cheekbones of the Aisin Gioro clan. It wasn't a handsome face as much as it was a face of authority.

"You are the Son of Heaven, Imperial Majesty."

It was explanation enough.

"You weren't so afraid of me the first time we met."

I was more uncomfortable with this informal tone than when he was agitated with me, so I didn't answer. There was no way to win when sparring with an emperor. Best to focus on the task at hand.

Taking hold of his arm, I carefully folded back the long sleeve and pressed two fingers to his wrist.

"The imperial physicians have been worthless. If nothing else, you have a woman's touch."

I fought to keep my hands steady. That was not how an emperor spoke to a nameless servant, which is what I wished to be right now. His gaze burned into me while I continued to search for his pulse.

"There is nothing irregular," I reported. "I will try to balance the flow of qi at the source of the pain."

"Go on, then."

Yizhu closed his eyes once more and laid his head back as I selected a long needle. The tail was capped with silver and the body tapered as thin as wire. My hands steadied as soon as I positioned it between my fingers.

Holding my breath, I reached up to touch his cheek. Using two fingers, I pulled the skin tight and inserted the first needle just to the left of his nose.

The Emperor didn't flinch. The points were so fine and the contact shallow enough that there was no pain. I continued with the next needle.

"Better," he said after I had set most of the points on his left side. His breathing had slowed, grown deeper.

"This treatment is only temporary. His Imperial Majesty must resolve the source of the imbalance to truly eliminate the pain."

"Resolve the source." His lip curled, and the flow of energy through the needles faltered. "Can you tell the Emperor how to remove the foreign devils from our ports? Or how to crush the rebel armies ravaging the countryside?"

"That is beyond my capabilities, Imperial Majesty."

"Beyond my greatest generals as well, it seems."

He fell silent, but tension gathered along his spine and through his shoulders. A muscle ticked along his jaw.

"Breathe," I reminded him softly, hoping I hadn't overstepped my bounds.

The Emperor exhaled, and I measured the pulse at his neck before adjusting the needles. The next set of insertions traveled along his neck. Yizhu remained still and silent while I worked.

When I glanced up from the task, his eyes were open once more and looking directly at me.

"When I was a child, I remember exploring the workrooms of the Ministry of Science. A young girl once dared to reprimand me."

My face heated. I moved to his other side and said nothing.

"My attendants were quick to drag the child from my presence and have her beaten for her insolence. That little girl was the chief engineer's daughter."

My father had been one of Yizhu's tutors. It was too much to hope that he'd forget, as the Emperor never forgot any transgression against him, no matter how small.

"Not many have ever dared to correct me in such a fashion, Physician Jin."

Yizhu's mood seemed to twist about like a snake in the grass. For all I knew, he was just trying to amuse himself. I longed to be done with this task so I could go, but I didn't dare rush through it. One wrong point could mean my head.

From outside the hall, a crier announced the commencement

of the daily court hearings. I froze, startled the Emperor would have me here during official proceedings, but he seemed to think nothing of it. The members of the Grand Council filed in, each sinking to his knees in a kowtow before rising to take his assigned place before the dais.

Most of them were senior members of the court, of whom I knew nothing aside from the rank denoted by their headdress and court robes. The youngest of them, however, was easy to recognize. Yixin, prince of the first rank, bowed before his half-brother.

Yixin was younger than the Emperor by two years. A bout of smallpox during childhood had left his face pockmarked, though he was otherwise not unattractive. At eighteen years, he had the same slender build of his half-brother and the same aristocratic features, down to the stubborn set of his jaw. The Emperor's mirror image.

These were the men who controlled the fate of the empire, and I was completely out of place here.

A functionary approached the Emperor to present a booklet with the first petition. My heart raced as Chen Chang-wei entered the audience hall along with an elder official.

It had been months since I'd last seen Chang-wei, and we'd only chatted briefly about my brother's studies. Our respective positions kept us apart, but I didn't realize until then how much I looked forward to seeing him. A chance meeting felt like a gift.

To my eyes, he was notably handsome, with well-defined cheekbones and a strong chin that tapered slightly. His eyes had a way of taking in everything and cutting it down to its component parts. Outwardly, he was well studied and well mannered, but he had a thoughtful expression that promised a thousand untold secrets.

I couldn't look at him without feeling a tug deep in my chest, but I knew it was just a faint echo of the past. Of the life I'd once been meant for. We had at one time been promised to each other, but the arrangement had fallen apart with the rest of my world when my father had taken the blame for the empire's defeat at the hands of the foreign devil ships.

It was rare for me to see him in full court dress. He and his companion wore the dark blue robes of the Ministry of Science with a Mandarin square embroidered onto the chest. Chang-wei's insignia displayed a peacock in blue and green thread. His work developing gunpowder fuel for the imperial fleet had earned him a promotion to scholar of the third rank. The other man, who appeared at least twenty years his senior, wore a white crane. First rank and Chang-wei's superior.

Though I had never been formally introduced to the head of the Ministry of Science, everyone in the palace knew of Kuo Lishen. The chief engineer had headed the construction of the palace fortifications, including the steel dome that encircled the Inner Court.

In unison, the two men bowed and pressed their foreheads to the ground before rising. Yizhu caught my hand as I started to withdraw.

"Continue," he commanded.

Chang-wei glanced up from the foot of the dais, and his gaze fixed onto me. I could see the question in his eyes before he looked away. My face burned as if I'd been caught in some scandalous act, even though I was here by the Emperor's command.

I had no choice but to do what I was told. Picking up another needle, I pressed my thumb against the meridian on the side of Yizhu's neck to stimulate the flow of qi. I could feel his voice resonating as he addressed Chang-wei.

"What is your request?"

"Imperial Majesty, we have received a communication from the Empire of Japan," Chang-wei began.

"Not a direct communication," Chief Engineer Kuo interjected.

The force of his interruption caused Yizhu to raise his

eyebrows. Chang-wei tightened his jaw but remained silent in deference to his superior.

"It is from an old signal tower, which hasn't been in use for over ten years," Kuo argued.

Yizhu let out an exasperated breath. "Then why come to me?"

"At one time our two nations collaborated on a scientific endeavor, attempting to connect across the sea," Chang-wei argued.

"That was under the direction of the former head of the ministry," Kuo pointed out. "His intentions might have been . . . misguided."

He was speaking of my father. My hand froze on the Emperor's shoulder. I quickly removed it, but not before Chang-wei saw it. An unreadable look flickered across his face.

He continued impassively. "I believe the scientists in Japan still wish to make contact with us. We should send an envoy."

"Japan has little to do with our empire-," the Emperor proclaimed.

"Indeed, the island nation has reduced the number of our ships allowed in their ports by half," one of the senior chancellors reported.

"His Imperial Majesty is wise to be wary of our neighbor," Kuo practically crowed. "The Japanese emperor has been less than amenable to us. There are other more pressing matters that require the ministry's attention."

"Then send only one representative," Chang-wei insisted.

"Engineer Chen wishes to volunteer?" Kuo remarked snidely. "That is no surprise."

"The chief engineer should speak more plainly," Chang-wei returned, his voice tight. "If he wishes to make an accusation."

"Merely an observation." Kuo continued to direct his statements to the Emperor rather than to Chang-wei. "It seems Chen Chang-wei is always -concerned with what happens outside our land than within it."

Tensing, I waited for Chang-wei to defend himself, but he remained controlled-. "The empire of Japan can be a useful ally, Imperial Majesty. They've gained enough knowledge of the West to develop defenses against them."

"Their empire couldn't possibly have anything superior to your fleet, Son of Heaven," the chief engineer boasted. "We have already constructed a hundred airships with a hundred more to come. By his Imperial Majesty's own orders, gunpowder fuel production has increased by three times."

There it was. Pride. It was disloyal to even hint at a flaw in the system. A pang struck me because of what such production meant for us. More factory fortresses in the south, spewing smoke and fire. Men, women and children scoured from the fields to work the assembly lines. My brother, Tian, had narrowly missed being conscripted when we had returned to Peking instead of remaining in our village. He was only ten years old now. He'd been nine then.

The Emperor listened impassively to the argument between them before sighing in agitation. He lifted a hand to rub his temples. I rushed to hold back his sleeve so it wouldn't upset the needles.

"When my father was Emperor, no one dared to bicker in front of him. Like quarreling children."

Both men fell silent.

"For a thousand years, the islands of Japan were a tribute state to our empire. Then Japan began to think of itself as an equal." Yizhu's lip curled. "We have no need for them."

Chief Engineer Kuo bowed, looking satisfied with the Emperor's decision, but Chang-wei would not be silenced.

"Though Japan cannot match us in power or greatness, they are close neighbors," he insisted. "The islands have been closed off to our empire for the last hundred years. Would it not be beneficial to firmly establish the Emperor's status as ruler of the greatest empire? It will not be long before the *Yingguoren* infiltrate the islands and attempt to gain a foothold. Western traders already have a settlement there."

"Like how the foreign devils have insinuated themselves into our ports?" Yizhu asked cuttingly.

His hand gripped the arm of the throne so hard that his knuckles turned white. Hastily, I started to remove the needles. With his temper rising as it was, the acupuncture would do him no good.

"Japan remains untouched, Imperial Majesty. We should establish ourselves as an ally. We can present a unified front against the Western nations."

Surely Chang-wei had to know how dangerous his line of reasoning was becoming, but he stood his ground without wavering. I had to admire him for it, but I feared for him as well. I knew what happened to men who contradicted the Emperor of China.

"Imperial Majesty." Prince Yixin's voice was noticeably quieter than the other speakers, but the room immediately stilled. "A visit may be worth considering. Japan is a close neighbor. Their thinking must be closer aligned with ours than with the West."

The Emperor regarded his half-brother silently. It was said that Yizhu was chosen as crown prince over his brother because the young prince didn't harbor the same hatred of the foreign devils.

"Enough." Yizhu shoved my hands away as I finished removing the last of the needles. "I will consider your request," he said impatiently. "That is all."

The men bowed and retreated from the throne room while the attendants escorted me out through a much less auspicious side door.

I hurried to the courtyard to catch Chang-wei. He was in conversation with Engineer Kuo but caught sight of me out of the corner of his eye. As the senior official moved on, Chang-wei hung back as I crossed the expanse of white stone.

"Engineer Chen."

"Miss Jin." His expression remained hard.

"It was unacceptable for Chief Engineer Kuo to speak to you like that."

"He can do whatever he wishes. He's my superior." Chang-wei continued walking as if disinterested, but I saw how his shoulders tensed. "The Grand Council considers me a Western sympathizer and a traitor merely by association. They'll never trust me."

"They should trust you," I said, angry for him. "Most of them have never been outside the walls of Peking. They're like frogs in a well."

"It's not important." He stopped, shaking his head. "Miss Jin. Soling, what were you doing in there?"

His quiet question caught me off guard. "The Emperor summoned me."

Chang-wei regarded me for a long moment before nodding. A nod that didn't look like acceptance or approval. He resumed walking, keeping his gaze ahead.

"I have no choice if the Emperor commands me," I insisted, upset that I had to defend myself at all.

His jaw clenched tight. "As you say, the Emperor commands us all. His will is law."

Chang-wei believed in defending our land, even if he had to sacrifice himself. This was the first crack I'd seen in his loyalty to Yizhu, and it wasn't over the empire.

I reached out to take hold of his sleeve. "I don't seek any special favor."

He finally met my eyes. "Be careful, Soling. That's all."

With that, he bid me farewell. I had forgotten that we were in public, before the watchful eyes of palace interlopers. Once Chang-wei was gone, I looked back over my shoulder and saw another face I had not seen in a long time.

Inspector Aguda wore no insignia on his robe, but his presence within the Inner Court told me he had retained a trusted

position in the new regime. He was a member of the Emperor's
Forbidden Guard, dispatched for the most critical of missions.

Aguda bowed once in my direction. I returned the greeting
warily before turning to go. The feeling of uneasiness stayed with
me long after I left the shadow of the dome.

2

I woke up the next morning long before sunrise, as I always did. The apothecary was dark and silent as I lit the stoves and brewed the herbal medicines.

The maidservants gave nothing away when they came to retrieve the trays for their respective mistresses. It wasn't until I started my rounds in the imperial harem that I discovered something was wrong.

With my acupuncture case and medicine bag in hand, I headed to concubines' palace. It was a complex of private courtyards and apartments surrounded by gardens.

I was told the Xianfeng Emperor's harem was a modest one, in terms of numbers. Not due to personal restraint, the eunuchs explained, but because the imperial treasury had been depleted in recent years—due to the extravagance of our previous sovereigns, these eternal servants were quick to point out.

The concubines' palace was surrounded by a wall, and the single entrance was through a narrow gateway guarded by eunuchs. I passed through without incident.

Sometimes the ladies would congregate outside in the garden

or sit beneath the shade of the pavilion, painting or embroidering. Today, the first courtyard was empty.

I went first to Imperial Concubine Li's apartments. No one had been named Empress Consort yet, but Concubine Li held the highest rank—which meant Yizhu had paid her the most attention. Her apartment was the most spacious of all the concubines', and she was assigned the greatest number of maidservants.

Two of her attendants stopped me at the door to her chamber. "Madame Physician."

I suppose I appeared matronly to these maidservants. They were young, many of them brought into service just out of childhood.

"Imperial Concubine Li is indisposed at this time," the maidservant explained.

I nodded and promised to return later. On selection day, Yizhu had chosen eighteen potential consorts, with two additional girls selected from palace servants who had caught the Emperor's eye. Visiting all of them would take up the next few hours.

The consorts of the fifth and sixth rank were housed in the west wing. Their quarters were smaller, though still lavish compared to mine.

Noble Lady Lan occupied a chamber at the far side of the courtyard with a window facing a plum tree. Her attendant had just finished combing and pinning her hair as I entered.

"I've been waiting for you," she said.

Her greeting took me aback. Every morning, I came and went like a servant. None of the ladies ever paid me any attention.

"Are you well, Noble Lady?"

"As well as can be expected."

She studied my every movement as I approached before gesturing toward the chair opposite her. It took me a moment to realize she was inviting me to sit.

"Please, Physician Jin," she said when I started to protest. "I only ask for a little of your time. I know you must be busy while I"—she looked around her sparsely decorated chamber—"I have nothing to do but wait."

She fixed me with a rueful smile, and I found myself complying. Lady Lan was younger than I was; seventeen or eighteen at the most.

"You're surprised I know your name," she stated. "I knew from the start you were not like the other servants. Your family hails from the Eight Banners, does it not?"

It was an old designation, harkening back to the armies that had fought alongside the great Nurhaci to found the dynasty.

Her hands were folded primly in her lap, and she held her shoulders straight. Unconsciously, I had mirrored the very same posture. Such careful upbringing was hard to erase, even though my family had been banished from Peking for eight years before returning.

"My ancestors were descended from the Bordered Red Banner," I replied.

"I was right. You are no ordinary servant," Lady Lan murmured. "My family is of the Nara clan."

One of the ruling clans of the empire.

"Your father was a ranking official, was he not?" the lady pressed on.

Again, my father. Every mention of him opened up a fresh wound.

"He was no one of importance."

"Now you're lying." Her gaze sharpened on me, narrowing like a cat preparing to pounce on its prey.

"I'm being humble, as befits my station," I countered.

Her lips twitched at that. Lady Lan wasn't an obvious beauty, but there was a certain spirit about her. A directness that could have been seen as overly bold or simply honest. Her gaze was piercing and bright.

"Your *station* could have been in here, with the rest of us,"

Lady Lan pointed out. "Yet you were assigned to the physicians' court."

Was this why the other concubines looked at me with such scrutiny and suspicion? Did they truly think I was yet another rival?

"I'm not of noble blood," I protested. "Nor do I possess the training or upbringing required—"

"The Emperor summoned you yesterday," Lady Lan interrupted.

"He required the skills of a physician."

The Forbidden City was ruled by routine. Whenever the routine was altered, people began to talk. I should have known the Emperor's summons would cause gossip.

Noble Lady Lan smiled for the first time, though it was a cold one. "Ah yes, most of us are waiting for a single glance from the Emperor, let alone to be summoned to His Imperial Majesty's presence."

Heat rose up my neck. "The Emperor had a headache."

"Our Emperor has a whole court of imperial physicians, and yet the Son of Heaven summoned you. Quite an honor, wouldn't you say?"

I had formed a sense of these women over the last year. Though many were content to patiently wait in hopes of catching the Emperor's notice, a few were ambitious to rise in the ranks. Noble Lady Lan was one of those.

"I always wondered why you were assigned to the harem," she confessed.

"A female physician is more knowledgeable of a woman's needs."

Lady Lan shook her head. "Do you really think that's the only reason? The eunuchs in the Court of Physicians perform their duties well enough. What needs do women have that are so mysterious only you can attend to us? Why not some matronly woman with years of experience raising daughters and grand-daughters?"

The conversation had my teeth on edge. I hadn't come to Peking to be dragged into the power struggles of the imperial harem.

"Two of the concubines were once maidservants, elevated directly to the fifth rank on the Emperor's whim," she said with a trace of bitterness. Lady Lan was only of the sixth rank herself. "It upsets the balance, this choosing based on a moment's fancy. But none of us fear them. They are not fit to be Empress or even hold the rank of noble consort, even if they bore the Emperor a son."

She leaned closer, as if taking me into her confidence. "One needs allies in the Forbidden City, Physician Jin. The difficult part is, which one of us should you befriend? Any one of us could be Empress one day. Or we may simply fade away as old maids, in the Palace of Forgotten Favorites."

"I am here at the service of the imperial harem," I replied firmly. "With no other aspirations."

"Nonsense." She teased and scolded at once. "Everyone in the Forbidden City has aspirations. Do you know the eunuchs here gamble as well? They consider which one of us will be chosen. Who will be the mother of a future crown prince?"

I could imagine her pressing the palace eunuchs in the same manner, searching for any advantage. I glanced at her attendant, who remained in the corner, his expression unchanged. He was better trained than I.

"The truth of it is no one thinks a concubine of the sixth or fifth rank will ever catch the Emperor's eye, let alone become Empress," she went on. "Most think Imperial Concubine Li will become Empress one day. She's the most beautiful of us, is she not? The Emperor certainly prefers her company. But you and I know it takes more than mere beauty to capture the Emperor's attention."

First Chang-wei and now Lady Lan. Emperor Yizhu's sudden

interest in me was threatening to become the inner palace's latest scandal.

"Noble Lady Lan, I don't seek the Emperor's attention in the way you speak."

"Apparently, you already have caught his interest. You have spent more time alone with the Emperor than many of us here in the harem, his chosen consorts. Our Emperor seems to find it appealing to break protocol. All men desire a challenge. A conquest, even if they have no need for it."

"It is not my wish to interfere in any way."

"I believe you, Physician Jin. As you admit, you are not prepared to play this game. But I am." She declared it with such certainty that I was taken aback. "In the meantime, you have the Emperor's regard. As temporary as it may be, that is worth more than silver and gold. That is the reason for my offer."

"Your offer?"

Now she did smile openly. "Of my friendship, Physician Jin. It will be much more valuable when it's the friendship of an empress."

Gossip of my visit to the Emperor spread quickly. The Emperor's eye was wandering again.

It didn't matter if the rumors were true or not. I had been summoned. I had been brought privately before the Emperor. Even Chang-wei had looked at me differently afterward.

By the end of the next double hour, I had seen everyone but Imperial Concubine Li. As I neared her quarters, a familiar scent hung in the air. I stopped short.

It was opium smoke, both bitter and sweet at once. The air was tainted with it. The same cloying smell used to come from my mother's chamber every day. It clung to her clothes and hair, and even though she hadn't touched it for a long time, I knew she still craved it and the forgetfulness that only opium could bring.

The black poison was everywhere now. Even the Forbidden City wasn't immune to its lure. The palace eunuchs and even ranking officials indulged in their pipes, but this was the harem. Imperial women were strictly regulated. Emperor Yizhu would be *furious*.

Her maidservants remained in position and glanced at me nervously as I approached. Ignoring the protests, I started to push past when the doors swung open. One glimpse of the golden-robed figure inside, and I fell to my knees. The maidservants behind me did the same.

"Is that you again, Miss Jin Soling?" the Emperor drawled.

"Imperial Majesty," I murmured, keeping my head down.

My heart pounded as he approached. The Emperor never came to the harem. Protocol dictated his consorts be brought to the imperial bedchamber.

"I never properly thanked you for your service yesterday."

He sounded sleepy, as if wading through a dream. I started as Yizhu leaned over to personally help me to my feet. Though it could be taken as insolent, I raised my eyes to his.

His pupils had shrunken to two black pinpoints. My heart sank, disappointed.

When not raised upon his throne, Yizhu presented a less than imposing figure. He was of average height and slight of build. Behind him, I only saw four guardsmen in his entourage.

I realized I had stared at the Emperor for too long when his slack, contented expression suddenly hardened. "Does harem physician have something to say to the Emperor?"

Yizhu was standing close, crowding me in the narrow corridor. Around us, the rest of the gathering remained with their foreheads to the ground. The Emperor's retainers stood back, silent as statues.

"Nothing, Imperial Majesty."

"I don't think I believe you," he said slyly.

He had backed me up against the opposite wall, but I didn't dare put a hand up to stop him.

"Imperial Majesty, I implore you." I lowered my voice and forced it to remain steady. "There are others here, watching—"

"So let them watch." Yizhu's smile was almost cruel as he fell into informal address. "I can do anything now, you know. I can have history rewritten."

The imperial court regularly condemned the opium trade, even though we were forced to allow it. Seeing Yizhu like this broke my heart. He had made a vow to fight the *Yangguizi*. He had promised to learn from this father's mistakes, but a very different man stood before me now.

"Opium is a . . . a dangerous remedy, Imperial Majesty," I warned.

"Have you ever tried it, Miss Jin?"

My palms began to sweat as he leaned in even closer. "I haven't—"

"Isn't it the way of things now? We must allow the poison inside, let it fester until we grow strong enough to expel it. Just like the *Yangguizi* growing rich in our ports."

I started to reply about foreign devils and how all of the imperial edicts prohibiting the sale of opium would amount to nothing if the Emperor himself were addicted, but I never had a chance to speak. Yizhu's fervor cooled as quickly as it had come.

"It's wonderful," he continued languidly. "The headaches, the pain, every single care goes away. I can appreciate simple pleasures once more: food, wine, beautiful women."

The heat of his breath fanned against my cheek. The Emperor caught my wrist as I tried to slip past, and I froze. His grip was iron around me, and he was the Emperor. To raise a hand against him meant death.

"*Radiant Highness.*" A soft purr came from behind him. Over Yizhu's shoulder, Imperial Concubine Li peeked out from the doorway. She held out her hand and beckoned to him playfully. That seemingly careless gesture communicated her status to everyone present. Yizhu was at her beck and call. "The Emperor's most dutiful servant misses him dearly."

The Emperor dropped my hand as he turned to her, grinning. The drooping look of contentment took over his face once more. He went to her without a glance back. Relief flooded through me.

As the Emperor took Imperial Concubine Li into his arms, she tossed a pointed look at me before the double doors were pulled shut.

BY THE TIME I returned to the shelter of the apothecary, I was exhausted, but there was no time for rest. A shipment had arrived from the trade bureau. A stack of crates had been deposited into my workroom, and it was a welcome distraction. Here was a problem I could solve. It didn't involve power struggles or palace intrigue or a young Emperor's whim. I scanned the manifest before settling in to work.

The physicians' court received a constant flow of spices, tribute teas and herbs from the provinces as well as a few rare remedies from the merchant ships. The more valuable shipments were usually snatched up by the head eunuchs and either kept for the Emperor's private use or distributed to members of the Grand Council in exchange for goodwill.

I was left to sort out the more common remedies. One of the crates was marked with an unusual seal. I didn't recognize the trading house, and when I searched through the manifest, the contents were listed as tea. There was no record of purchase. This had been sent as a gift.

Inside was a sack filled with dried flowers. When I pulled out a handful of the blossoms for a closer inspection, a rain of tiny black seeds scattered over the table. *Yingsu* poppies, the same flower that yielded opium.

I ran my fingers over the petals, and a few flaked off. The curious thing was, we had plenty of *yingsu* in our drawers. The plant had long been used for medicinal purposes. The flower and seeds, and even parts of the stalk, could be boiled down into a soup to dull pain or aid digestion.

But somewhere along the way, it was discovered that the resin extracted from the seed pods was a hundred times more potent. And when the substance was smoked rather than swallowed, its darker, more addictive nature emerged.

Why had this crate been sent when we had a steady supply of it? It wasn't until I lifted the sack that I saw the woodcut engraving on the bottom of the crate. It was an ocean junk, triple-masted with battened red sails to catch the wind.

I knew this ship. I had spent several weeks on board over a year ago. Apparently its captain hadn't forgotten.

I emptied out the rest of the sack and inspected every board and nail on the crate, searching for a message. There was none—Yang Hanzhu wouldn't be so heavy-handed. He was wanted for treason. Any communication between us could put me in danger, yet he'd still managed to secretly smuggle a shipment into the Forbidden City.

Yang had been a chemist in the Ministry of Science under my father. Everyone who knew him thought he was brilliant. He was also a bit of a scoundrel. Once he'd been loyal to my father, but now he was loyal to no one.

The poppies lay in a pile on the worktable. *They* were the message. Opium came from a plant we had known and used for over a thousand years. It had been transformed into the black poison that now infected our country. And somehow, for reasons we didn't yet understand, it had been transformed again.

Yang was still searching for the answer to opium, to the addiction, and to the strange sickness we'd seen evidence of firsthand.

The afflicted fell first into a deep sleep from which they couldn't be roused. But if they did awaken, they became like wild animals. Pure instinct, unadulterated rage.

When I'd first been installed in the palace, I'd written petitions to the Ministry of Science, to the trade commission. I sent accounts from Changsha about the opium sickness, for which I received no answer.

I shuddered as I thought of how many doses of opium were being set to pipes at this very moment. How many addicts lounged inside opium dens scattered throughout the capital? Whorehouses, teahouses. The imperial palace itself. They all craved the black poison, breathing the smoke into their lungs. Inviting the demon inside.

That evening, I was awoken by another messenger. The Emperor suffered from a headache and needed my services. I brewed the herbal potion and sent it on before crawling back into bed.

For the rest of the night, I tossed and turned in my bed, waiting. I expected the Emperor's servant to return with an imperial decree that I was not allowed to refuse.

The decree never came, but I was convinced one day it would. Not because I was particularly pretty or charming or clever. It would come because Yizhu was Emperor and I was a conquest. One that he could win.

3

I n the Forbidden City, there is always the danger of being swallowed whole. Of being buried deep and forgotten.

That was how I felt when I sent a petition for an audience with the internal office of security the very next morning. When there was no reply, I sent another request the following day. And another the day after.

It was like shouting from the bottom of a deep and narrow well.

At one point, I even considered writing to Chen Chang-wei. Certainly he would listen to my situation. He would help me.

In the end, I tore up the letter. Chang-wei was an engineer.

A week had passed before I received the summons from the head of security. The moment I had the letter in hand, I headed to the imperial guard headquarters. There I presented the document to the stone-faced guards out front, half expecting to be turned away. Without a word, they stepped aside.

There were guardhouses stationed throughout the palace, but the central office handled the bureaucracy of managing the thousands of bannermen in the service of protecting the Emperor.

The headquarter building was fashioned of dark wood,

unpainted and lacking the gilt and ornamentation of the audience halls. When I was led into the headman's office, however, it
was more akin to a scholar's study than a soldier's hideout. A
carved cherrywood desk anchored the room, and the walls were
bare except for a map of the inner palace that spanned the far
wall. Various sections were marked with colored flags.

Headman Aguda adhered to the old Manchurian custom of
retaining a single given name. He stood from his desk as I
entered.

"Miss Jin Soling," he greeted.

His height made his bow appear awkward, though he moved
with a measured, almost stately grace. When I first met him, he'd
held the rank of inspector and was part of the crown prince's
inner circle. A member of the Manchurian elite. Aguda was the
one who had sought me out, looking to recover my father's
secrets.

That last mission had given the empire a formula for
gunpowder fuel, one that was currently used to power its engines.
In return, Emperor Yizhu had officially cleared my father's name,
allowing our return to the capital. And Aguda was promoted to
head of the imperial guard.

So I wasn't completely without allies within the Forbidden
City. I wouldn't call the headman a friend, but we had history.

I wasn't accustomed to seeing him in the robes of a ranking
official. His embroidered square showed a tiger with claws bared,
and his cap was set with an ostrich feather.

"Do you realize that a petition within the inner palace typically takes weeks, if not months, to be processed?" he asked me,
eyebrow raised.

Aguda's lips twitched as he tapped a hand against a stack of
papers. I recognized my writing on the petitions. Whatever it was
I had expected from this meeting, it wasn't humor.

"What is so urgent, Miss Jin, that you had to come see this
humble servant?"

"I came to express my sincere gratitude, Headman Aguda, for my current appointment. And to ask humbly if I may be reassigned."

He arched a thick eyebrow. "Reassigned? That hardly sounds like gratitude."

"I know, sir. And I apologize, but the current position no longer seems . . . appropriate."

It was impossible to say what I was truly afraid of aloud. Yizhu was Emperor, and we all served him, but I didn't want to become a diversion, something to be used for the Emperor's pleasure and then discarded.

"I owe you a debt of gratitude," he began quietly. "It is because of your valiant efforts that the Emperor saw fit to promote me. For that reason, I saw fit to help you in any way I could. A position within the inner palace, in close contact with the Emperor and the imperial court. Is that not a great honor?"

"In close contact with the Emperor's concubines," I corrected.

His eyes gleamed. "Don't underestimate the importance of your work. Those women comprise the secret court in the palace, Miss Jin."

"It is a very important position, sir. But . . ."

I could see the way Yizhu had looked at me, more with cold determination than interest. And how the imperial harem and palace eunuchs looked me differently as a result of the emperor's regard. I had become a player in their game.

"This is not the fight I came here to fight," I told Aguda boldly.

"I thought your temperament would be well suited toward this assignment. You're observant, levelheaded. Not quick to become involved in any disputes. It was only a matter of time before people came to trust you, and yet you yourself trust no one."

How had I not seen this before? "You wanted an informant in the inner palace."

His gaze pierced into me. "Nothing as insidious as you make it sound. It's good to have eyes and ears everywhere. For security purposes."

"But—" My mind was spinning. "You never discussed any such plans with me. How would I ever know to report to you?"

His lips twitched. "Are you not here now? Tell me, is there any truth to the rumors about the Emperor's indulgences? His appetites in the bedchamber?"

I stiffened. "I know nothing of it."

"Nonsense, Miss Jin. You know everything." He rose from the desk and stretched to his full height. I had to tilt my head upward to meet his gaze.

"I know nothing."

His eyes bore into me. For a moment, we were locked as if in combat. Inside, my heart beat so hard I thought I would faint, but outwardly I remained calm. A skill I had learned from my time within the palace.

"Very good." I thought I saw a smile crack through the hard line of his mouth. "It would be a serious offense to find an appointment I had secured was passing gossip."

The headman relaxed, but I couldn't.

"I don't wish for you to be a spy, Miss Jin," he said, coming to stand before me. "There is no effort needed on your part. It would be just like Canton."

Just like Canton. In Canton, Aguda had set me out as bait.

My stomach knotted. I had the distinct feeling of being a frog in a well, able to see only the waters around me. "You deliberately assigned me to the harem to catch the Emperor's eye?" I asked slowly.

"As a favor. A young woman of marriageable age would find it a great opportunity. Certainly one that the Emperor knows by name. And our Emperor has shown himself to have a wandering eye. Granted, you are slightly older than most of the chosen concubines, but I figured it was only a matter of time."

I felt sick. Aguda had been trying to play matchmaker in some twisted fashion. "Please have me reassigned, Headman Aguda."

"And where do you suggest?" he replied coolly. "The physician's position in the harem may not be to your liking at the moment, but some of your other pursuits have cost great men their reputations—and their lives."

Other pursuits? I was close enough to his desk now that I could see two stacks of papers arranged neatly on it. One contained my requests to come see him, but the other stack was also in my handwriting. It contained petitions I'd written nearly a year ago. Ones I assumed had been discarded.

"Opium is an unfavorable endeavor," he said gravely. "We all know what happened to Commissioner Lin when he tried to eradicate the drug in Canton."

The commissioner had seized over twenty thousand chests of foreign opium and proceeded to burn it. And he'd started a war.

Lin had later died in exile.

As I glanced over my petition to warn the public of the tainted opium shipments, I noticed the character for *epidemic* had been blotted out with black ink.

"An unfavorable endeavor," Aguda echoed beneath his breath. "The harem is at least a harmless assignment."

"It's not harmless."

If we didn't have history, I wouldn't have dared to turn my back on him then. I had to leave before I let my temper get the best of me.

When I returned to Peking, I vowed I would not be bent to anyone's purposes. If living within the palace walls required that one live in a web of intrigue, then better I seek employment as a washerwoman along the riverbank.

"You should reconsider, Miss Jin," Aguda called after me. "Most would find it an honor to serve the Emperor. A consort enjoys much more privilege than a humble acupuncturist."

More privilege, but certainly not more freedom. Not in the way I saw it.

"The Emperor has selected many suitable consorts for his harem," I replied. "I can serve him best elsewhere."

I was a subject of the empire, but I belonged to myself, mind and body. I had earned that much. I had earned it.

4

On nights of the new or round moon, the inhabitants of the palace flocked to the temples of Jingshan Park. I took advantage of the full moon to venture outside the walls to the grass-covered expanse to the north.

A weight lifted from my shoulders the moment I was free of the Forbidden City. Of the iron cage and the legion of guards. Every breath felt easier, cleaner. I needed the sky above. I needed time to think.

Carrying a lantern with me, I followed a steep trail to the northern peak. The rocky hill was man-made, as was the rest of the park. The imperial engineering corps had used earth dug up from the surrounding moat and transformed it into a mountain. A small-scale mountain, at least, dotted with shrines.

A viewing pavilion rested at the peak of the slope. I climbed to the top and was happy to find it waiting, empty. From inside, I could see just beyond the palace to catch glimpses of surrounding Peking. The walls of the Summer Palace rose at the edge of the city borders. One palace wasn't enough for our Emperors. This was another fortress. Another show of splendor.

An airship rose lazily above the palace grounds, just edging above the horizon. Its belly must have been laden with cargo that slowed its ascent. I watched the sails billowing as they caught the wind.

The vessel resembled one of the great treasure ships that had sailed the oceans during the reign of the Ming Emperors. Perhaps that was done deliberately to evoke the same sense of grandeur and conquest. Only a few generations ago, our empire had ruled the seas.

Unfortunately, the *Yangguizi* weren't as mindful of history or traditions.

"One would think you were eager to leave, Soling, the way you watch them go."

I turned to see Chang-wei clearing the top step. The twilight sky beyond framed him in shadow, but I would recognize him anywhere from his silhouette alone. From his lean frame and strong shoulders to the tilt of his head. Chang-wei always held himself with such thoughtful poise.

He settled down beside me on the bench, and for a while we just watched the airship rise up into the clouds. The silence between us was easy, comfortable, like a warm blanket. For a moment, it was like it had been when we were traveling the southern province together. I hadn't realized how much I'd missed this.

"It's been a year since we landed in that airfield," I remarked.

"Hard to imagine."

We used to watch the ships take off from the airfield together, speaking about the wide world outside of Peking, but lately there had been little opportunity. Chang-wei's duties kept him busy, and I was being drawn deeper into the complexities of the inner palace.

"Peking has changed so much, I barely recognize it," I went on.

"Every Emperor adds glory to his name by building," Chang-wei remarked. "At the end of his reign, the Daoguang Emperor threw his efforts into fortifying the city."

"And our Xianfeng Emperor builds war machines," I finished for him, referring to Yizhu's reigning name.

For the last ten years, the factories of the south had churned out weapons and ships, powered by coal and iron from the mines. If we'd remained in our village, my brother would have likely been conscripted into the factories. The frantic push to produce had put a strain on the population, which had, in turn, pushed more peasants and laborers into the rebellion.

"The walls and the towers, I can understand." I had glimpsed the Western merchant fleet docked in Canton and Shanghai. The iron monsters lined our shores, fitted with their cannons and steam engines. The memory left me cold with dread.

"I had always thought of the palace itself as a grand and beautiful place," I said. "A place where great things happened."

"You're inside now. Everything looks different from inside."

"Sometimes I fear—" I looked to the horizon, past the walls and towers and fortifications. We were so enclosed inside the Forbidden City. "Sometimes I fear I'll forget the things we've seen outside of the palace if I stay inside there too long."

I thought about telling him of my petition to be transferred from the harem. Would he consider me ungrateful? Or worse, disloyal?

"It has been a while, hasn't it?" Chang-wei asked quietly.

"One becomes isolated in the Forbidden City."

"But not forgotten."

Chang-wei was an anchoring presence beside me. When he leaned close, I could smell sandalwood on his robe. It was the scent of books and libraries and ancient scrolls kept in locked cases.

There was something I needed to know. "You left so quickly the other day."

Chang-wei averted his eyes on the guise of watching the airship. "There are always eyes watching in the palace."

"What did you not want them to see?"

My heart stood still as he glanced back at me. Chang-wei's composure was a thing of legend, but his confounded look at that moment was almost endearing.

Gently, he reached to brush back a strand of my hair tugged loose by the evening breeze. His fingertips just grazed the shell of my ear. Each movement seemed drawn out and deliberate. At least time seemed to have slowed for me.

"There are things that have happened between us," he began. "Things that make me irrational at times."

Was now one of those times? The first and only time we kissed had been a situation like this. We were atop the citadel in the city of Changsha during the rebel siege. We had been alone up there before Chang-wei rode out with a garrison to defend the city.

He'd kissed me. And I'd kissed him back, forgetting all the chaos that swirled around us.

We were alone again now.

I turned on the bench to face him, fighting to keep my breath steady. But Chang-wei remained where he was.

He gazed at me thoughtfully. "I overstepped my bounds in the Inner Court the other day. When I saw you, I reacted out of emotion."

"And how else can one be expected to react?"

He went on, unfazed. "The Emperor is our sovereign. If he had . . . he can have anyone he wants—"

"It's not like that," I cut in.

Why was I blushing? I hadn't encouraged the Emperor. And truly he hadn't shown any interest aside from a few simple requests. Treatments for headaches. For sleeplessness. When considered in bright daylight, there was nothing unreasonable about his demands.

Yet there were stories told by the eunuchs. Our Emperor was young, virile. The stories claimed he had a taste for the forbidden: dancers, servants, perhaps even the daughter of a disgraced official?

His exploits were hardly for me to judge. I knew of another Yizhu. One who had studied diligently under my father. One who woke at first daylight to attend to the empire's affairs and stayed awake late into the night fretting about uprisings and foreign devils and rebels who were tunneling under city walls and beheading Manchurian officials.

Yizhu was my Emperor, and his purpose was my purpose. But he was also a man pulled in directions. Perhaps he couldn't be blamed for drowning himself in pleasure for the few moments that were his own. But I was determined not to become one of those conquests.

Overhead, the airship turned southward, trailing a faint plume of gunpowder smoke. It passed to the east, avoiding the grounds of the Forbidden City. The low rumbling of the engine split the air like thunder.

"Where do you think this one is going?" I asked as the roar of the engine faded. I didn't want to talk about the palace anymore.

"Perhaps it's being sent to supply to troops along the Yellow River. Or to reinforce the fleet in Changsha," Chang-wei surmised. "The imperial army has started using the walled city as a base for further attacks against the rebels."

"Yang Hanzhu escaped from Peking on the Ministry's old airship," I remarked, not knowing exactly why I thought of the chemist at that moment. "He escaped the purge along with several others."

Chang-wei's mood darkened at the mention of his former colleague. "Yang has always been resourceful."

"Would you have gone with them?"

"It doesn't matter. It wasn't possible."

Chang-wei had been captured at the battle of Wusong and

imprisoned on a ship captained by the *Yangguizi*. After my father took the blame for the empire's loss, his corps of engineers and scientists had been scattered, but Chang-wei alone returned to the Emperor's service.

"I tried to continue Yang's opium experiments," I confessed. "But the head physician wouldn't allow it."

In the evenings, I wrote down all I could remember of the experiments I had conducted on Hanzhu's ship as we'd analyzed different opium samples. Yang Hanzhu had been convinced opium was at the heart of the empire's decay. I couldn't argue with him on that. Even if the *Yangguizi* were chased out, and the rebels defeated, our empire would still be infected.

Yang theorized that something had made the substance more addictive. That it had been altered in some way.

"I proposed such a study to the Ministry of Science as well," Chang-wei admitted. "But Minister Kuo rejected the notion. There's no glory in such experiments. He prefers to sponsor building projects on a grand scale so the court can shower him with praise."

"While opium is an unfavorable endeavor," I murmured.

The drug was a black mark upon the empire. It left everyone's hands unclean.

After being apart for so long, I was afraid we would be strangers again, but here we were, falling into our old patterns: Chang-wei discussing his dreams for the empire; me listening intently, wondering if this is what our lives would have been like if fate had been different.

When I'd returned to Peking, I thought we would continue as we had before. Chang-wei and I fighting for the empire. Together.

The airship had become a smudge against the clouds, fading quickly into the evening sky.

"Will you be watching when my airship takes flight?" Chang-wei asked.

I turned to him, startled. "Where are you going?"

"To see our neighbors on the island empire of Japan."

My eyes grew wide. "The Emperor decided in your favor after all."

"Several days ago, Chief Engineer Kuo changed his stance and argued on my behalf. Nothing like an adversary's support to make one doubt oneself."

It was the first time Chang-wei had called Kuo Lishen a rival. "You think the chief engineer has some other purpose in mind?"

Chang-wei shrugged. "Perhaps he merely wants me out of sight for a while."

Despite his loyalty to the empire, Chang-wei still struggled for acceptance. There was a time when I had doubted him as well. Even though I considered him a friend, there was so much I didn't know about him. What had happened during his time among the *Yangguizi*? And why did he continue to maintain contact with Westerners in the treaty ports?

But all those questions faded away as the realization of what he'd just told me sank in. "How long will you be gone?"

"It's uncertain. A few weeks, perhaps a month."

I hugged my arms to myself, suddenly feeling cold. "That . . . that isn't too long, I suppose. Hopefully it will be an uneventful journey. Are airships as tossed by storms as the ones in the sea?"

I was unable to focus my thoughts. Chang-wei watched me with a look that was part kindness, part confusion, and I wanted to swallow my own tongue to keep it from babbling.

He was my only friend in the capital. I was feeling more trapped inside the inner palace every day, and now Chang-wei would be leaving as well.

"Do you truly believe an alliance with Japan will help us?" I asked.

His expression became thoughtful. "The Ministry used to exchange ideas with scientists in Japan, but not since your father left and Kuo took his place. Their studies took a different direction than ours. The study of firearms."

"From the *Yangguizi.*" Just the mention of the foreign devils left a bitter taste in my mouth.

"Not everything from the West is evil, Soling."

I didn't respond. The war against the *Yangguizi* had cost my father his life. I would never trust them.

"Japanese knowledge with our factories to produce the weapons," Chang-wei went on. "I'm not a strategist or a general, but it seems logical to me. Combine the efforts of our two nations against a common adversary. The Westerners haven't attacked Japan, but it's only a matter of time."

"The Japanese won't think kindly of you if you go bearing that message," I warned.

Chang-wei always forgot about politics and human pride. In his head, the world was a logical place where people would be compelled to make the right decisions if allowed to see them.

In truth, people had the right decisions in front of them all the time and still chose wrong.

"Airships and war vessels won't solve all of our problems. Chief Engineer Kuo has risen through the ranks by feeding the court's hatred and fear of the *Yingguoren*. His solution is to build higher walls around the ports," Chang-wei said, agitated. "A dome around the inner palace to prevent attack. A greater army. Everything is focused within, like a tortoise retreating into its shell. It can't be the only way. We have to look outward."

"I hope you're right," I murmured. "I really hope you are."

When I had returned to Peking, it was upon one of the Emperor's dragon ships. For the first time in eight years, I had looked upon the city of my birth with hope. Chang-wei had given that to me.

"The Emperor refuses to consider an alliance with a nation that is beneath him. And Chief Engineer Kuo won't abide by any ideas but his own."

"Yet they are allowing you to go."

He smiled faintly. "Chen Chang-wei on another one of his mad schemes."

A wave of loneliness hit me. I wanted very much to be a part of his mad schemes. I had come to the capital to be a part of the fight, but now Chang-wei would continue with his battle, while I remained tucked away, hiding like a tortoise in its shell.

5

I tried not to think too much of Chang-wei leaving. It would drive me mad.

Instead I absorbed myself in my duties in the physicians' court, and the next days passed by uneventfully. I heard nothing else from the Emperor. Hopefully he'd forgotten about me.

By the time I was to take my monthly leave, the natural rhythm and routine of the harem returned.

Outside of the Forbidden City lay the Manchurian section of the city. My mother had found lodging in a modest courtyard house among the winding *hutong* alleyways. I was given leave once every month to visit her and my brother.

The mechanical sedan chair took me through the palace gates and along the prescribed path through the streets. I always looked forward to these visits away from the protocols and rituals of the palace. Every time I saw my younger brother, I was reminded of exactly why we had come back to Peking.

The property was not much larger than ours had been back in the village. It was comprised of three rooms around a central yard. Nothing like the mansion our family had once occupied in

Peking, but that place had been long taken over by some other official. I wouldn't have remembered if it I saw it. That time was a lifetime away from who we were now.

But life had been good to us, all things considered. I drew an imperial salary now, and I sent my earnings to my family. My brother Tian was promptly enrolled into one of the imperial academies after Chang-wei personally presented him to the headmaster. How could the academy refuse when Tian was sponsored by a prominent member of the Ministry of Science? For the first time in years, all things seemed possible.

My duties in the Court of Physicians had taken on a comfortable routine. I knew the eunuchs looked upon me as an outsider, but the work kept me busy. I had hundreds of herbs and ingredients to study and memorize. The imperial records were also fascinating. I pored through historical records of elixirs given to Emperors. Elixirs of crushed pearl and mercury, meant to increase virility. Even grant immortality.

It was easy in the shelter of the palace to believe there weren't foreign devils living among us. That the empire wasn't being torn apart from inside by rebellion. But I couldn't forget. At night when I closed my eyes, I could see the ports of Canton and Shanghai clogged with foreign ships. I could hear the explosions that shook the walls of Changsha.

I wouldn't let myself forget.

As I approached the gate of my mother's home, a man with his cap pulled low nearly collided with me. He only glanced at me before departing without apology.

The door of the front room was open, so I entered without needing to knock. Mother was seated over a satchel of papers. She straightened abruptly when she saw me.

"Soling, I had forgotten you were coming today." Her hands fidgeted, touching the portfolio and retreating. There was a lacquered box beside it.

"Where's Nan?" I asked, glancing at the slim case warily. Our maidservant was always about, but I couldn't hear her in any part of the house.

"I sent Nan to the market for a few things. She should be back soon. How are you, Daughter?" Mother spoke in a rush, all her words strung into a single sentence.

"I'm well. And you?"

Without even thinking, I searched for the signs. The shades were drawn, and Mother was certainly nervous. The pupils were the easiest way to tell if she had taken a pipe, but she was avoiding my gaze.

Immediately I felt guilty. It had been over a year since Mother had touched opium, yet every time I came to see her, I was in fear that she'd weakened and returned to it.

Mother glanced furtively at the lacquered box before redirecting her gaze to me. "I needed something to keep me busy. Especially when your brother is away at the academy."

Once more, she grasped the edges of the portfolio, straightening it in front of her. What had my mother so agitated?

"What's in the box?" I asked, bracing myself for the worst.

"It's not what you think, Daughter." With a sigh, she opened the case to reveal a series of brass dials inside. "It's a calculating machine," she explained when I continued to stare at it without comprehending. "It's been years since I used one of these."

Her hands caressed the dials almost lovingly. I had only recently learned that my mother had once been a candidate for the imperial science exams. An oddity, since the exam was only open to men.

"The Ministry requires some calculations for their building projects."

I sat down beside her as she opened the portfolio and rifled through the papers. Each one was covered with mechanical drawings and symbols. After a few pages, my eyes swam.

"Do you understand all of this?"

"Understand it? In many ways this is clearer to me than language."

Her expression was dreamlike. Disturbingly, it was not entirely unlike an opium trance, though her eyes were focused.

"Engineer Kuo brought this to me." She straightened the papers and carefully placed them back inside the portfolio.

I was taken aback. "Kuo Lishen? Why would the chief engineer come to you?"

"I sent him a letter a few days ago." Mother sighed. "Soling, I've been in a waking dream for so many years. It's . . . it's difficult to be back here, in this city. And to have to see everything and feel everything. To not be able to close my eyes."

I knew it was hard for her to talk about the past.

"Peking is no longer our home. I don't know if we have a home anymore. And the days are so long now. They stretch on forever. We get by from the money you and Engineer Chen provide, but—"

"Chen Chang-wei gives you money?"

She looked surprised that I hadn't known. "For Tian's studies."

I remembered Chang-wei mentioning he would help my brother when we reached Peking, but I had thought he meant securing him entrance to one of the science academies within the capital.

"We have to give it back."

Mother didn't argue with me. Instead, she smiled faintly. "So you understand why I contacted Kuo. I asked him if there was any way I could be of service to the Ministry. I was trained in the scientific branch of the Hanlin Academy, did you know? I would have passed the exams as well, if it weren't for . . ."

Her voice trailed away, and she looked sullen. As if a light sparked within her for only a moment before slowly fading away, starved of oxygen.

"Old Liu Yentai told me you were a gifted mathematician," I told her gently.

She touched her finger once more to a brass dial on the calculating machine. "We didn't have a calculating machine in my father's shop when I was growing up. When I first came to the Academy, I used only an abacus. But I was faster than most of the other candidates. Confucian scholars insist it is wrong for a woman to take such glory, to boast about her accomplishments, but it was mere fact."

"You met Father at the Academy?"

"I met your father at the Academy." She folded her hands before her. Her tone sounded faraway and wistful. "I met Kuo Lishen as well. We were all candidates for the exams, can you believe it? Your father had already failed one attempt. Kuo had failed twice. I believe the examiners at that time expected one to fail. They wanted to select candidates that were determined enough to come back. Science is inherently rife with failure, Soling. Failures and retrials."

It was strange to hear her talking like this. Not like the mother I remembered as a child or the stranger who had been confined to her room, her eyes glassy and opium smoke filling her lungs.

She sounded almost like my father used to when he spoke of his work at the Ministry. In front of me, their conversations had been brief. Reports of what happened that day. But what had their conversations been like in private?

I fell silent, eager to hear more of Mother's secret past—which was apparently only secret to us, her children.

"When I was discovered, another candidate threatened to expose me. I had to leave the Academy and pursue a different life, but I still loved numbers. When the figures come together, when they balance out, there's indescribable beauty in it. Peace."

She closed the lid of the calculating machine gently, as if it held her most precious jewels.

"So you asked Chief Engineer Kuo to give you work?"

"I was so proud of you when you were appointed to a position within the palace. Envious and proud." She reached out to tuck back a strand of my hair, and I stiffened, then immediately felt bad for doing so. But Mother continued. "Kuo said it was impossible to employ me at the Ministry. Too many people there knew of my marriage to your father—and of the unfortunate incidents that happened."

His execution. How the Daoguong Emperor had condemned him. Even though Yizhu had promised to officially clear Father's name, people still remembered.

"But Engineer Kuo said there was work I could do for him outside the Ministry. Rote work, he admitted. But I was grateful for the chance to do something useful again. So he brought the machine and these designs here."

I remembered the man who had run into me at the door. I'd only caught a glimpse of his face, but had that been Kuo Lishen?

"The chief engineer came himself?"

Mother nodded as if it were nothing.

With secret documents and some hidden task. I didn't like that one bit. "Let me see those plans again."

I opened the portfolio to look through the drawings once more, but they were as cryptic to me as they had been upon first glance.

"What is this really, Mother? Why does Kuo need you to work on it outside of the Ministry?"

"It's in pieces," Mother explained, trying to keep the pages in order as I rifled through them. "There are entire rooms full of retainers calculating such sums in the Ministry."

I thought of how Kuo antagonized Chang-wei, but did that make him a villain? Mother knew more about the chief engineer than I.

"It's good you've found work, Mother," I said instead.

"It is good," she agreed, tapping the calculating machine. "When I was at the Academy, I dreamed of a different life, solving

important problems on a grand scale for the Emperor. But everything changes so quickly, Soling. I'm fortunate Engineer Kuo
remembers me from before. I suppose it would be hard for him to
forget."

"Was it Kuo who threatened to expose you back then?"

"Hmm?" Mother glanced up from the papers. "Oh no. It was
your father who made the most trouble for me. He was a man of
strict morals and honor, even then."

~

I STAYED AWHILE LONGER, sharing tea with my mother. She was
absorbed in the new work Chief Engineer Kuo had commis-
sioned, and I could tell she was eager to start.

Nan came back from the market with a sack full of yams for
the evening meal. I handed my silk purse of coins over to her,
which she pocketed without a word. This silent exchange was
routine between us. Mother didn't look up from her formulas,
though she was well aware of what was happening. I don't think
she even trusted herself with money.

My brother returned from the Academy close to sundown.
Tian was ten years of age now, and more serious every year. He
gave the calculating machine a curious glance before setting
down his books beside it.

"Greet your elder sister properly and wash up for
dinner, Son."

Mother ran a hand over his crown before going to see to Nan
in the kitchen. The easy affection between them caught me by
surprise. In the past, it had always been my brother and me,
clinging together. It was another sign that time had passed. That
we were all different now.

"*Nín hǎo*, Soling," he mumbled.

"How are your studies, Brother?"

"Well, Elder Sister."

"You seem taller."

He shrugged and said nothing. Tian was sprouting like a bamboo reed. His face was thinning out as he lost the roundness of youth, which made him look more and more like father.

Supper was in the common room, and the three of us sat around the square tables like we always had. Mother plucked pieces of yam into my brother's bowl, and they exchanged words quietly to each other.

I couldn't help but feel I was intruding. "How are your tutoring sessions with Engineer Chen?"

"He's a good teacher." Then, after a pause, "He asks about you."

My heart skipped a beat. "Often?"

Mother glanced up. What made me ask such a foolish question?

"Not often," Tian amended, causing my spirits to plummet.

I couldn't linger for too long after dinner. My leave only allowed me until sundown to return to the palace. I bid my farewell to my family, promised to return in a month as I always did and said the usual parting words.

"Study hard, Tian. Take care, Mother."

They stood at the door with Nan just behind them as I set the controls of the sedan. As the machine whirred to life, Mother gave a small wave before putting her arm around Tian to lead him back inside.

A wave of loneliness swept over me as the wheels of the sedan began to turn. My family was growing closer, while I was drifting away. Though we'd been poor in our village, though we'd been hungry and fearful, it was what we knew. There was a strange comfort in that.

But our lives were better now because I worked in the palace. Much better.

I looked over my shoulder to the house at the end of the lane and watched it until it disappeared.

THE SUN WAS SETTING as the sedan passed through the east gate into the imperial city. A functionary stood just inside, watching my approach expectantly.

He bowed once. "Physician Jin Soling, you have been summoned."

I was immediately ushered into a carriage that set off out through the gates once more. I watched the streets fly by outside the carriage window, and my stomach knotted as we moved beyond the walls. We were leaving the inner city.

An airship came into view in the distance, the distinctive red balloon visible against the orange dusk. We were headed toward the Summer Palace.

Dark rumors floated about the Summer Palace. This was where the Emperor had women brought to him. Dancers, entertainers, Han women with their bound lotus feet. Women who were unsuitable as consorts, yet no woman was truly forbidden to the Emperor.

I knew Yizhu wasn't as depraved as the eunuchs made him out to be, but I grew nervous as the carriage neared the palace grounds. I had never been summoned to the Summer Palace. The celebrations and rituals there were meant for the highest ranked of the Emperor's subjects.

The airship loomed large with the dragon's head carving clearly visible at the prow. A symbol of the imperial fleet. The carriage passed through the outer gate with armed guards monitoring the passage from the watchtowers.

Rather than heading into the palace proper, the carriage veered west toward the airfield. My curiosity ran wild.

The imperial court often gathered for the launching of the dragon ships, but as we neared the vessel, there was only a small retinue of imperial guards. Everyone else appeared to be airfield staff or crewmen.

Headman Aguda stood at the dock, still and foreboding. He nodded toward me as I stepped down from the carriage.

"You're late, Miss Jin," he said, coming toward me in long strides. "The ship nearly left without you."

I stared up at the billowing red sails and the great balloon frame filled with hot air. The gunpowder engines rumbled within the lower gondola. Thick cables kept the airship tethered, but the dragon was straining against the anchors, vying to fly free.

Aguda held a scroll out to me, and, in a daze, I reached for it, not yet comprehending.

"Your new assignment awaits." His lips twitched as he gestured toward the rope ladder.

My heart pounded. There was only one airship mission I knew of scheduled to embark this week. Chang-wei's diplomatic mission to Japan.

Tentatively, I placed a hand upon the rope ladder. An attendant came to help me onto it. I hugged the scroll tight to my chest as I clung to the rope. Bit by bit, I was hoisted up toward the deck.

Chen Chang-wei was there, staring at me in astonishment as I climbed on board.

"So this is our late arrival?" A middle-aged man in imperial uniform, who I assumed was the captain, stood next to Chang-wei.

I handed him the scroll. "Sir."

My voice caught in my throat. Chang-wei's gaze bore into me, seeking explanation. Unfortunately, I didn't have one to give.

"Physician Jin Soling." The captain looked from the scroll to me, then back. "Every ship has need of a good physician. Especially in foreign lands."

He didn't sound convinced. Nevertheless, an official decree was not one to be questioned. A moment later, he gave the order to free the ropes.

Chang-wei regarded me without blinking. "Soling."

"Chang-wei."

For the moment it was just the two of us, face-to-face, as the crew prepared to lift off.

"I'm glad you're here," he said finally.

I glanced back down to the ground as the airship began its steady rise. Headman Aguda lifted two fingers in an informal salute.

"I'm glad as well," I murmured.

From the outside, it might have looked like Aguda was showing me favor. I had asked to be reassigned from the harem, and here I was. But everything the headman did was for his own gain. If he put me on this mission, it could only mean it served his plans.

Aguda needed eyes and ears on this airship. And the likely target of his attention was Chen Chang-wei.

6

Captain Zhao worked to accommodate my presence, instructing the crew to clear a cabin. When I came to my temporary lodging, a satchel had been placed upon the sleeping berth. Someone had packed my personal belongings inside: a folding leather case containing acupuncture needles, a kit of medicinal herbs.

There was little privacy in the palace, but the thought of Aguda or his minions going through my room made my skin crawl. But I'd been granted freedom. At least for the moment.

By the time Chang-wei came by, we were high up in clouds. The sky outside my window was a dark, inky swirl, penetrated dimly by the guide lanterns fixed around the hull of the airship.

"Were you aware of this?" Chang-wei asked.

"I was summoned directly to the airfield. I requested a new assignment, but I never thought Headman Aguda would bring me here."

With Chang-wei. My pulse pounded excitedly.

Chang-wei raised an eyebrow. "You asked to be reassigned?"

"I had to do something. The Emperor. The way he—" It was too difficult to explain.

The details were unimportant. The important thing was that I could breathe easy now. I didn't have to worry about being caught in some palace scheme or unwittingly attracting the Emperor's notice.

Chang-wei nodded, but his expression remained distant. Thoughtful. He closed the cabin door and pulled a stool up beside the bed.

"You don't seem happy about this," I prompted as he sat down. I was a bit wary of the situation myself.

"No. No, this is good. This is useful."

I was unconvinced.

Chang-wei finally met my gaze directly. His tone changed, and he became all business. The serious scholar and official I'd come to know.

"Diplomatic visits to Japan are not permitted," he explained. "Only trading ships are allowed into Nagasaki, and only the ones that have been properly sanctioned."

"And this airship?"

"Captain Zhao has a long-standing agreement with the trading houses in Nagasaki. I'm posing as a physician being brought in to treat the inhabitants in the Chinese foreign settlement."

"So it makes perfect sense for me to pose as—"

"As my wife," he finished. "This was good thinking on Aguda's part. Perfect sense."

His reluctant tone told me he wasn't quite convinced, either. "This isn't the first time Aguda has tried to use us for his schemes."

"But he's not here now. It's just you and me," I assured, even as suspicion gnawed at me.

"The Grand Council doesn't trust me."

"I trust you."

Chang-wei was unquestioningly loyal to the throne. He had convinced me the empire's struggle was our struggle.

He seemed to relax, though only slightly. "There's no need for them to worry. My motives are clear for anyone to see. I want to propose a collaboration. Simple."

"What sort of . . . collaboration?"

The choice of word was strange in and of itself. I knew little of military matters, but a nation that had kept itself in isolation for several hundred years wasn't likely to change within the course of a single visit.

"The empire of Japan has developed weapons that can be of use to us. Advanced firearms, based on Western designs."

I moved to the edge of the berth. "Will guns be enough to defeat the *Yangguizi*?"

"It's not the foreigners we're fighting." His tone took on a grave note. "A larger threat comes from within. The rebel army is advancing on Shanghai."

"*Heaven and earth.*"

An army of thousands had besieged us in Changsha. Miners and laborers and peasants who were tired of being enslaved.

"They've grown stronger since we faced them."

"If they're able to take Shanghai—"

"Then nothing will stop them from marching on Peking."

No wonder Yizhu was troubled day and night. A year ago, the rebel army had failed to take the city of Changsha, but the neighboring strongholds were not so fortunate. The rebels had modified the heavy machinery taken from the mines and factories and turned them into war engines. Cities crumbled beneath their assault. With each victory, their numbers swelled.

"We don't have the strength to hold off the *Yingguoren* and fight the rebels at the same time. The Emperor agreed to establish contact with the Japanese scientists. They might be willing to work with us."

"But it's dangerous. We're forbidden from going there."

He nodded. "This is not an official diplomatic mission, nor am I authorized to offer an alliance. The Emperor still believes his empire vastly superior to Japan. We are not to be seen as paying tribute."

It was a fine line to walk, but Chang-wei had experience striking such a balance. He'd lived among the Westerners for years.

"You said that we had received a message from the Japanese," I prompted. "Are they expecting us?"

"There's no way of knowing. Your father once maintained unofficial communication with the several scientists through the trading port in Nagasaki. He would send envoys a few times each year to exchange information. Near the end—"

He stopped suddenly and looked up at me, apologetic.

"It's all right." The pang of grief was only momentary. "Continue."

"Near the end of your father's life, he managed to establish communications across land and sea."

Chang-wei reached beneath the bunk and produced a wooden box and a scroll, which he set down between us. I shifted back to allow him room as he spread out the map.

Realization struck me. "This was your cabin, wasn't it?"

He must have moved out hastily, leaving his belongings behind. "Your comfort is more important than mine," he said with a smile. "I can sleep anywhere."

I smiled back at him. I had missed this feeling of being close to Chang-wei, of sharing confidences. I remembered then that he was lending money to support my brother's studies. I needed to speak to him about that, but now was not the time. I didn't want to be indebted to him.

Chang-wei returned his attention to the map. "The empire of Japan has limited all foreign trade to two settlements here in Nagasaki."

The empire of Japan consisted of a string of islands curving to the east of the Joseon peninsula. Chang-wei indicated a location at the southern tip of the chain.

"There isn't as great a distance as one would think between Nagasaki and Peking. It can be traveled by sea in less than a week. By airship, in less than two days. My research through the Ministry archives uncovered mentions of a project to build a signal tower in Peking."

I knew immediately where the tower was located. "The Observatory."

Chang-wei nodded. "Among the instruments."

I had seen the Ancient Observatory when we'd arrived by airship. The platform had been built upon the ramparts of the old city wall and featured a series of astronomical instruments and structures cast in bronze and steel. At the center was a spire that rose high into the sky. I'd assumed it was yet another device for measuring the heavens.

"I first thought of it when I saw the device inside your father's puzzle box. I knew the box and device were Japanese in origin, but I didn't recognize its purpose."

Both Chang-wei and I looked to the wooden box set between us. The exterior was lacquered to a glossy black finish but otherwise unadorned. Chang-wei slid open the lid to reveal a drum of twisted copper wire and other metallic parts. My father's device was among them.

"It's a receiver. It took me the entire year consulting with old diagrams to fix the signal tower. Once it was operational, I started to receive messages."

Fascinated, I peered into the box. Chang-wei leaned in close, pointing out the metal plate with a cylinder attached. "The listening device attaches here. We should still be close enough to the tower."

Wires extended from the receiver to connect to an earpiece in the shape of a dragon. The device curled around my ear, attaching to form a cuff above the lobe.

A series of faint clicks came from the piece. "How do you know someone is sending this message?"

"The signal comes and goes, but I'm convinced the pattern starts to repeat after two hundred and fifty-six signals," Chang-wei explained. "I've written it down here."

He showed me a page of his notebook where he'd recorded a series of dots and dashes. I listened closer to the signal, searching for the pattern, but I was more aware of Chang-wei, head bent beside me, as we embarked on this new mystery.

"I haven't been able to decipher any of it," he confessed.

He had made an appeal to the Emperor based on a mysterious message he couldn't interpret? I hated to admit I was as skeptical as the Grand Council.

"How do you know the message is an invitation? It could be warning us away."

Chang-wei was adamant. "The tower was built in collaboration with the Japanese. Someone is signaling us, trying to start the conversation. We can't ignore it. This is what your father started, Soling. This is what he dreamed of. An exchange of ideas."

The way he spoke of my father touched me but also made me nervous. My father, the former head of the Ministry of Science, had been executed when the guard towers and cannons had failed to protect our key port cities from falling to the *Yangguizi*. Much later, I learned the reasons weren't so black-and-white. He'd written a report criticizing the empire's technology and defenses as inferior to the inventions of the West.

And now Chang-wei insisted on going down the same path.

I dropped my voice low even though we were alone in the cabin. "It was those ideas that labeled him as a traitor."

"But the flaw was not in his way of thinking. And Emperor Yizhu is different from his father."

That was true. Yizhu hated the *Yangguizi* even more than his father had, but Chang-wei was too idealistic to realize it.

I stared down at the coded message. Listened to the faint clicks coming from the receiver. Did my father's associates on the other side even know he had been executed a decade ago? Did they realize their signals had been lost to the sky?

Until now.

"The transmitting tower resides in Nagasaki, the only port open to our ships," Chang-wei went on with growing excitement. "Someone is trying to reach us there. We can't send a message back, but we can find the tower. We can reestablish contact."

"What happens when we find this person?"

His eyes shone bright. "Then we will no longer be alone in this fight."

THE AIRSHIP WAS a falcon-class transport vessel, more lightweight than the war-class ships and designed for smaller supply runs. From what I could see, the envoy consisted of Chang-wei, a translator, an armed escort of four Forbidden Guardsmen and now myself.

The vessel flew through the night with the engines purring beneath us. I tried to get what rest I could. As Chang-wei had promised, by midafternoon as I strolled the upper deck, I could see land in the distance. Were we truly so close to the island empire?

"Come see the harbor." Chang-wei beckoned me to the side.

A wave of dizziness struck me as I looked down and gauged how high we were. The coastline below was barely visible through the clouds.

The countryside was far away and quiet from up here. A feeling of awe swept over me just as it had when I had entered Peking in the Emperor's dragon airship. In the blue waters of Nagasaki Bay, I could see several ships, their sails the most visible feature from on high.

I also realized for the first time what a strategic advantage airships could serve. For the last several years, Peking had pushed the factories in the south to the breaking point manufacturing more. Mining crews had been worked to exhaustion to produce more ore. The number of vessels in the imperial fleet was carefully guarded. The Emperor didn't want our enemies to know we were gathering our strength.

As the airship gradually descended over the bay, I could clearly make out a fan-shaped island in the distance, just off the coast.

"Dejima, the Dutch trading port," Chang-wei explained, coming to stand beside me. His shoulder brushed against mine, and the year apart faded away. It was like this between us when we'd first arrived in Peking.

"Only a limited number of trading ships are allowed into Japan each year from each nation, and contact with foreigners is strictly controlled. Our empire is at least allowed a settlement on the mainland."

Several stone watchtowers lined the coast, rising high above the wharf. Chang-wei produced a pair of eyeglasses from the pocket of his sleeve and put them on. He adjusted the telescopic attachment over the right lens. Then he scanned the shoreline, his gaze sweeping over the entire bay before us. He seemed to be searching for something. With my naked eye, I could see the outline of the city and the rise of the hills beyond, lush with vegetation.

"This is when we find out whether our official request is in order. Captain Zhao is sending the signal now."

Up in the main mast, I could see flashes of light as the crewman angled the signal mirrors.

"We needed to get special dispensation to land an airship." Chang-wei handed the spectacles to me. It took me a moment to focus the eyepiece onto the watchtowers, at which time I could clearly see the cannons aimed at us.

"All should be well," Chang-wei murmured as I tensed.

I had a nightmare vision of crashing into the sea in a ball of flame. At that moment, an answering signal came from the nearest tower. I handed the spyglass back to Chang-wei. And then waited.

The boom of cannon fire never came.

"They're hailing us in," Captain Zhao reported.

I let out a breath and gripped the rail as the airship continued its gradual descent.

"Nothing to fear," Chang-wei said, reaching out to touch his hand to mine. The touch was brief, there and gone.

Chang-wei was always calmest when the danger was greatest. One of the defining characteristics I'd come to know about him.

"Are the Japanese hostile toward our empire?" I asked. From where we stood, we could be approaching one of our own ports.

"They have no reason to be. I have more to fear from my own countrymen."

I pondered his remark as I watched the coast come in closer. At first I thought he must have been speaking of the rebels, but it was odd for Chang-wei to refer to himself so personally.

We passed over Dejima, and I strained to catch a glimpse of the Dutch traders, but everything looked like miniature models from this vantage point. The people were as small as mice.

I had seen Western foreigners for the first time in the Shanghai settlement, even spoken to one who had taken the time to learn the Canton dialect, a trading language, common to many of the treaty ports.

Though they were pale skinned and lighter haired, I had to admit they were hardly devils. The differences in appearance were hard to focus on exactly. Some features such as the nose or mouth were larger and—I couldn't find the right word. *Coarser* in appearance.

Chang-wei was more familiar with the foreigners than most of our countrymen. He had been taken aboard a –Western ship after the first conflict. They'd forced him into service, and he'd even sailed all the way to their capital, a place called London, where he'd settled for several years.

I couldn't imagine it, living so far away in a strange land. The islands of Japan seemed a far-off and exotic place.

The landing field was marked by flags raised onto bamboo poles. It was located inland from the shore. Captain Zhao navigated the airship between the watchtowers and positioned it over the clearing. Air hissed from the jets as the balloon was depressurized, reducing the ship's buoyancy until it touched down on the airfield.

The airship rumbled as the captain cut the engines. The rotors wound down and went still. Down below, a Japanese entourage made its way toward us. They looked to be at least twenty men strong with swords that were sheathed, yet prominently displayed.

"Ready?" Chang-wei asked.

The look on his face was one of excitement. He was fully suited toward such adventure. The rest of our much smaller escort formed around us as the crew lowered the gangplank. I prepared to set foot down on the land of the rising sun.

7

C aptain Zhao took the lead, having made several landings in Nagasaki. "No political envoys or ambassadors are allowed to accompany the merchant ships," he reminded us as the port officials approached. They were escorted by armed swordsmen in case we presented any threat.

The captain greeted the landing party and explained our purpose, which was trade and nothing but trade.

Chang-wei briefed me on the details as we waited. Our cargo held ginseng and various other medicines and remedies. The landing party had been sent by the Saga domain, whose daimyo, the feudal lord, was charged with defense of the coast. I knew little of the samurai warriors of the Japanese aside from their legendary reputations for upholding honor until death.

As I glanced upon them now, I had the same sense of foreboding I felt among the *Jin Jun*, the Forbidden Guard that protected our Emperor. Among samurai, apparently one sword was not enough. Each man was armed with two. I supposed so they could kill a man twice, if needed. I kept my gaze directed downward.

Zhao provided papers and a circular jade seal that had been broken in half.

The samurai glanced at the papers and then back to the airship as if scanning it for weapons. He replied to the captain, and I found myself straining to understand, even though I knew nothing of the Japanese language. The sound of it was harsh to the ear, lacking the fluid tones of our tongue. He seemed to speak at great length, after which Zhao relayed a simple message.

"We will be escorted directly to the customhouse."

Captain Zhao brought two of his men, leaving the rest on board. Our party was five in number compared to twenty samurai who looked like they could cut us in half.

The foreign settlement was located along the shore. A stone wall delineated the foreign area, but the true boundary between Nagasaki and the trading post was enforced by the watchtowers that lined the coast.

"Separated by the distance it takes to fire an arrow," Chang-wei said beneath his breath.

We were allowed through the checkpoint with little incident given our armed escort. Once inside the trading post, the escort led us to an official-looking building set apart from the shops and stalls. The structure rose two stories high, and there were more guards at the front entrance.

It was the customhouse, and we were brought inside to be presented to the presiding official who sat behind a desk in the main room. Captain Zhao stepped forward with his seal. The official opened a box lying beside his papers and lifted another half seal, which he held against the captain's counterpart.

Once satisfied that the two halves fit together, the official gave a nod and pushed a ledger book forward. Zhao was familiar with the routine. He bowed once and bent to sign the book before gesturing to Chang-wei.

"Every foreigner registered and accounted for," Zhao remarked.

Chang-wei took the brush to enter his name into the ledger. As I wasn't asked to do the same, I assumed I had taken on the identity of his wife. It made us appear more respectable.

After registering at the customhouse, we were set free to roam the confines of the Chinese section. The settlement was filled with merchants' shops and stalls, not unlike the markets of Canton or Shanghai, but without the same crowded streets. There were fewer inhabitants here than on the mainland.

The buildings were constructed with two levels and inclined rooftops. Dwellings and shop spaces merged seamlessly together, and I watched traders haggling over prices in one shop while others sat down for steaming bowls of bone soup in the next. In the distance, I could see the curving rooftop of a temple, painted auspiciously red and rising above the clutter of the marketplace.

We walked along the main lane, feeling like strangers in this land despite the familiar sights. Stacks of porcelain ware filled one shop while another displayed bolts of dyed cloth. The language that flowed from the stalls was a mix of Chinese dialects and Japanese, reduced down to haggling terms and numbers. I saw a glimpse of silver change hands.

"The shogunate keeps careful control on who is allowed in and out of the country," Captain Zhao explained. "There is a strict number of ships from each foreign government and tight control over what goods are brought in. Customhouse officials are completing an inspection and inventory of our cargo at this moment."

"What of the opium trade?" I had to ask. So many of the ships leaving our ports were opium runners.

"Opium trade is banned by the Tokugawa shogunate and punishable by death."

"They must have taken warning from our struggles," Chang-wei remarked grimly.

Our empire would have been wise to do the same. If we had shut out the foreigners and executed the drug runners, we would be a different empire. Instead, the drug had flooded onto our shores in a black wave. Thousands upon thousands of chests of it. When we tried to close the gates, it was too late.

"Our ministry made contact with a foreign studies scholar ten years ago when we last visited," Chang-wei said. "He lives in Nagasaki city. Is there any way we can locate him?"

Zhao ran a hand over his beard. "I can make a request to the *bugyō* for a special pass outside of the Chinese settlement. But foreign merchants are low on the city administrator's list of concerns."

"I do appreciate your assistance, Captain."

With that, Captain Zhao left to oversee his business affairs. I watched him disappear into the market lane. "It may take a while before we can get the required passes."

Chang-wei frowned. "Hopefully there won't be too much of a delay. We don't have much time."

We went in search of lodgings and were quickly directed toward an establishment near the docks. There was a black-smith's forge nearby and a busy stable house. Though the inhabitants were in constant transition with traders coming and going, a permanent settlement had grown up around the port. To these people, Chinese quarter was home. The rest of us were strangers.

Chang-wei negotiated for rooms, and the only ones available were tucked in the back. They were small spaces stacked together, with a woven mat laid down as bedding and thin walls between them. Zhao and his crewmen took rooms in the north wing while Chang-wei and I occupied a separate apartment across the walkway.

I surveyed our chamber, which didn't take long. There was a bamboo mat laid down as bedding and a chamber pot for use at night. A screen separated out a private sleeping area.

There was a time I would have blushed to be in such close, intimate quarters with Chang-wei, but this wasn't our first adventure together.

He thought nothing of it, either. Putting on a pair of spectacles, Chang-wei slipped a tiny book into his palm. It was how he kept notes, using a trick from his student days of using a needle to write impossibly small.

"I imagine Captain Zhao's petition will gather dust on an administrator's desk," he said, flipping through the pages. "But the Chinese quarter isn't nearly as tightly controlled as the shogunate would have us believe."

"What if we get caught sneaking out?"

He was absorbed in his notes. "Probably tried as smugglers."

I shuddered, thinking of how sharp those blades looked and how the Japanese favored beheading as punishment.

"Perhaps there's another way," I suggested. "A safer one."

Chang-wei flipped through the pages. "I plan to send a message to a contact of your father's by the name of"—he squinted to read the characters—"Sagara. He's an aristocrat and a man of science. Reportedly supportive of an open exchange of ideas between our empires. He might make an effort to come meet us."

"How do we reach him?"

He consulted the notebook once more before snapping it shut. "Teahouse."

CHANG-WEI BYPASSED several large and busy teahouses near the inn, instead searching out an establishment in a quieter part of the quarter, down behind a row of warehouses. On the other side of the lane, I had seen dockworkers transporting crates, but as soon as we disappeared into the far side of the lane, the area became quiet.

"There's a proprietor by the name of Yelu with a modest teahouse in the warehouse section," Chang-wei explained.

"Do you think he'll still be there a decade later?"

"We'll soon find out."

We found the place. There was a lantern hung out front with a painted signboard with a fish on it. We entered through the thin curtain and found the main room empty of any customers. There were no hostesses or servers, either. Curiously, a set of dolls lined the walls of the room, each dressed in a differently colored kimono. Their faces were childlike, with pleasantly painted smiles. Each doll balanced an empty tray across its arms.

Chang-wei and I exchanged glances before seating ourselves, and it took me a moment to find a comfortable position on the floor. I had to shift this way and that and still didn't feel as if I was doing it right.

Tea came a moment later, but not from any human hand. A panel opened in the wall, and one of the dolls turned to receive a ceramic teapot onto its tray. The mechanical tea server then came toward us in tiny steps, stopping before our table.

Chang-wei lifted the teapot himself, at which point the server bowed, gears whirring.

"A windup toy." My father's colleagues from the Ministry had often given me such devices as gifts when I was a child. It was one of my fondest memories.

"Clockwork dolls," Chang-wei concurred.

As Chang-wei started pouring tea, a hostess finally entered the room. She wore a floral print kimono, and her hair was styled in an elaborate bun. In her hands, she held a stringed instrument. With a bow, she seated herself on the mat and prepared to play.

"Your doll is very charming," I told her.

"*Karakuri*," she replied. I didn't recognize the Japanese word.

The hostess was younger than I was by a few years, which would make her around sixteen or seventeen. I was enthralled by the vibrant pattern on her kimono, pale blossoms on a yellow springtime background. There was something both elegant and extravagant about wearing so much silk.

"I didn't realize there were Japanese women in the Chinese quarter." I took a sip from my tea and spoke in a lowered tone.

There weren't many women in the settlement. Most of the shop owners and traders had been men, which was probably typical of most ports. Traders left their families behind to make their fortune, coming home when business allowed it.

"The man we're looking for is named Lord Sagara. Yelu the teahouse owner was supposed to get a message to him," Chang-wei reported.

"You've mentioned two men by name, and you were able to find this place despite its remote location. How is that possible when you've never been here?"

"Your father kept a journal of his visit to Japan." He looked almost apologetic. "I've read the entries."

My pulse quickened. When my family was exiled from Peking, the imperial authorities had confiscated all of Father's documents. But they hadn't destroyed his research as we originally assumed. Instead Yizhu, then crown prince and now emperor, had studied it to search for a way to fight back against the Western invaders.

"I would return it to you if I could, but the journal belongs to the Emperor's imperial archives."

"Don't trouble yourself over it." I looked at Chang-wei. My father had chosen him to be my husband, but that was in a past life that was long gone.

"I could get permission for you to read it, if you'd like."

My chest hitched. He was trying so hard to be kind. "No, that won't be necessary."

Father's writings would be full of mechanical drawings and scientific observations. There wouldn't be any mention of me or our family. Though he had always cherished Tian and I, work was work. It was enough to see that a man like Chang-wei still honored his memory. Father continued to serve the empire, even in death.

During our brief exchange, the mysterious proprietor finally arrived. He appeared to be fifty years of age, with a face that was plump, pleasant and easy to forget. His jacket was fashioned from dark, high-quality silk.

He lowered himself onto the mat to address us face-to-face. I could see how this custom of sitting on the floor created a more casual, intimate atmosphere for conversation.

"Welcome, precious guests! Newly arrived, I see."

"Master Yelu?"

The proprietor bowed to acknowledge that was indeed his name.

"I hear this is the best tea in the quarter. Zhejiang tea."

Yelu's gaze flickered before being replaced with his previous affable expression. "The best. Dragon well tea."

"I prefer Dragon Mountain. But this is very good."

I could only imagine this banter was part of some coded exchange.

"I'm curious about the city beyond these walls," Chang-wei said.

"Ah yes. Nagasaki holds many wonders, friend. But the domain has become strict about who is allowed outside, or inside for that matter. The *yujo* I employ have work permits. Every night they are required to leave the settlement and return to the Japanese city."

The young hostess returned to place a plate of rice flour cakes onto the table before slipping silently away.

"The *yujo* are very good for business," Yelu remarked. "With many talents."

It was easy to assume he was speaking of their bedroom skills. I spared our Japanese hostess a closer look. The voluminous sleeves and wide sash around her waist could easily serve another purpose—smuggling items out of the quarter.

While the *yujo* played, Chang-wei and the proprietor continued to speak in a low tone, too quiet for me to hear. At some point, a folded paper appeared in Chang-wei's hand and promptly disappeared into Yelu's sleeve.

Afterward, we finished our tea and left coins upon the table.

"You're quite suited for this type of spy work," I told Chang-wei as we left.

"There isn't much to it. All one has to do is appear remarkably ordinary."

A smile played across his lips. He held his hand to the small of my back to guide me down the lane, and I could feel the warmth of his touch through my robe. There was nothing ordinary about Chen Chang-wei.

8

Dinner was at a bustling noodle stand that overlooked the docks. Every bench and table was full, and we sat elbow to elbow with traders and laborers. The mechanical arms of the noodle-pulling machines whirred at a blinding pace to keep up with the constant flow of customers. Snatches of conversation filtered through the hum, and I could pick out several dialects, the most prevalent being the Shanghai dialect.

From the diners and what I could see of the street, there were very few women. At least in this part of the quarter. What few I spied appeared to be like our song girl at the teahouse, Japanese women who came from Nagasaki proper to entertain in the quarter. *Yujo*, the proprietor had called them. Several of them entered a tavern at the end corner.

Our noodles came, and I turned my attention back to our surroundings. With the crowds around us, and the smell of scallions and bone broth in the air, I certainly felt I was back in our homeland.

Chang-wei was talking to one of the workmen packed into the table beside us. "Have you ever been to Dejima Island?"

"The Japanese are strict about keeping us separated. The Dutch settlement is completely closed off to us, just as they're forbidden to enter our settlement. The Western goods we do see come from Japanese merchants. Curiosities, mostly. Little trinkets and devices."

Chang-wei appeared intrigued. "Where can I find some of these curiosities?"

The man mentioned a shop nearby before digging back into his noodles.

The majority of the customers were head down over their bowls. This was a place to eat quickly, throw down a few coins and make room for the next hungry sailor. There was little talk, but I could hear snatches of conversation around me. Someone mentioned the rebel army and how it had moved farther north, spreading out to attack cities close to Nanking and Shanghai. A feeling of dread settled in my stomach. I wanted to believe that these were merely rumors, but for news to travel across the sea to the island empire, there had to be the weight truth of behind it.

I lifted egg noodles with chopsticks and scooped up some of the rich, salty broth. The street fare was satisfying in a way that warmed my heart as well as my stomach. Not that I would complain about the food from the imperial kitchens. My family had been through very lean times back in our village, and the southern provinces were still ravaged by famine. It was one of the reasons the rebel scourge was able to gain so many followers. I knew better than to complain about being fed at all.

Once our bowls were empty, we stood to go, and our spots were immediately snatched up.

"We should find this shop. There may be items of educational value," Chang-wei suggested. He asked for directions from a passerby, and we were on our way.

I tried to peer past the beaded curtain at the door of the tavern as we walked by, but it was impossible to see anything in the hazy glow of the lanterns. Laughter came from within, male and female combined, leaving the rest up to my imagination.

The shop we were searching for was down an alleyway. A painted signboard above the doorway indicated the name, and the shopkeeper was just closing his doors as we approached. Evening was creeping in, and most of the establishments were done with business for the day. Chang-wei was insistent. As he negotiated with the shopkeeper, I held back and peered through an opening in the alley.

It wasn't a proper shop or stall. Rather, the shelter looked like a place for squatters and hang-abouts. I could see a man reclined on a mat. Even in the dim light I could make out the long, slender outline of an opium pipe.

"Strictly regulated, indeed," I muttered as Chang-wei returned to my side.

Chang-wei steered me away from the den. "As I said, the quarter is not as tightly controlled as the authorities would believe."

Opium found a way to creep into every corner, rich or poor. Maybe it was a Chinese disease. Our own innate failing.

Once we were out of the alley, I noticed the bundle tucked beneath his arm. "What is that?"

"A souvenir." He looked immensely pleased with himself. "Something you'll like."

He'd gotten me a gift? I was feeling a little pleased myself.

WE RETURNED to our room at the inn and sparked the hanging lantern. Chang-wei then placed the paper-wrapped bundle at the center of the mat and stood back to let me open it.

"I paid entirely too much," he admitted. "But the old man was intent on closing the door in my face until I showed him a heavy purse."

Kneeling, I peeled away the brown paper to reveal a thick tome. The writing on it was unintelligible—which made my pulse skip with anticipation.

I turned the book around to open the cover, but Chang-wei stopped me. "They open it from this end."

"From the back?"

"And it reads from left to right."

"Interesting..."

The pages were thick and yellowed, and the characters on them were printed close together. The script appeared quite spare and simple. It might have been a book on shipping schedules, but it felt so mysterious in my hands. Full of hidden knowledge. My father had owned an extensive library of books he'd collected, but any foreign tomes had been translated into Chinese. The imperial court didn't allow Western books in Peking.

"Do you know how to read this?" I asked, turning another page with only my fingertips and taking care not to bend the corners.

"I've learned how to read the language of the *Yingguoren*, but this is from Dejima. It's written in a language called Dutch."

Chang-wei went to the window to call out to a passing street vendor while I continued to pore over the foreign volume. The next turn of the page had revealed an illustration.

"Have you figured out what the book is about?" Chang-wei had procured a pot of tea from the street seller. I heard the clink of the lid as he checked on the contents.

"It might be a book on astronomy."

"How can you tell?"

"These look like star charts."

I was so completely absorbed that I barely paid attention to Chang-wei setting tea beside me on the mat. He poured a cup and placed it into my hands. "Be careful of the book."

I wouldn't dream of spilling a single drop on it. Not in a thousand years.

The tea proved to be a bitter. Either over roasted or over steeped. I only took a small sip before setting it down to continue inspecting the book. There were a few notations in the margins in what must have been Japanese.

"I don't suppose I'll get a look until you're completely done?" Chang-wei asked.

I glanced up. He sat back with tea in hand, regarding me with a bemused expression.

"You can come sit right here if you want a closer look," I offered, a bit defensive. It wasn't as if I were selfishly hoarding the book or the ink disappeared as soon as I read the words.

"Actually, you enjoy it. I have some matters to discuss with Captain Zhao. Don't forget to drink your tea before it goes cold. The tea seller will collect the cups from outside the window."

I nodded, head back in the foreign book while Chang-wei left to go call on Zhao's quarters across the courtyard. Before I knew it, I had paged through a third of the book—which went quickly given I couldn't read the words. The illustrations, however, held a world inside each drawing. I studied every line with utter fascination.

By the time I took another sip, my cup had gone cold. I poured myself fresh tea from the pot to warm it, but I found the brew had become so bitter it was undrinkable. Curious, I lifted the lid.

A small satchel had been placed inside over the tea leaves.

I fished out the translucent packet with two fingers. Hot tea drained from it as I tore the cloth open. I recognized the contents immediately. Anyone who had mixed over a hundred sleeping potions in the imperial apothecary would know these ingredients on sight.

Scowling, I plunked the satchel back into the pot and shot to my feet. I managed to wrench the door open without tearing the delicate layer of paper. Zhao's room across the walkway was dark. Regardless, I went to knock on the door and received no answer.

Chen Chang-wei. The scoundrel. He hadn't voiced any objections when I had been added to the mission. No mention of *It's too dangerous* or *I don't want to get you involved, Soling*.

I was happy to see how much he trusted me. How he trusted my ability to take care of myself. Instead he'd resorted to drugging me while he headed off on some caper.

I was ready to snap bones. I was ready to spit fire.

That scoundrel hadn't been gone for long. I stormed out of the inn, pausing only to inquire with a few stragglers out in the street. Yes, they had seen the gentleman. He was heading down that street over there.

Gentleman. I could laugh.

The sky was growing dark, and lanterns illuminated the street corners. As I followed the twists and turns of the street, a nagging thought came to me that I was a young woman in a strange place where there weren't many young women.

I had my bladed fan tucked into my sash and my needle gun hidden beneath my mandarin jacket, but the weapons didn't make me feel any safer. I was just so mad at Chang-wei that I didn't care.

There was no sign of him in the streets. On a whim, I headed back toward the *karakuri* tearoom. The warehouses were deserted in the evening and cast dark shadows with too many invisible corners.

I slowed my step, preparing myself for danger as best I could. Out of the corner of my eye, I caught a flash of movement around the corner. There was no turning back now.

The figure was the same height and build as Chang-wei. He passed beneath a hanging lantern before slipping once again into the dark. I took a step forward only to be grabbed from behind. Strong arms wrapped around me.

Crying out, I clutched blindly at my attacker, jabbing at any part of him I could reach. His grip was a vise around me as he dragged me up against him.

"She's following you," he grunted as I struggled in his grasp.

He spoke with an accent, the tones slightly flattened. It took me a moment to realize his words weren't directed at me. Chang-wei returned into the halo of lantern light.

"She's with me," he said, alarmed. "Let her go."

As if on command, the stranger's arm slipped away. The man slumped to the ground and lay unmoving. Chang-wei stared at me, then at the body at my feet.

I removed the hollow needle hidden against my palm and glared at him across the alleyway.

~

"Who . . . is this?" I huffed.

The stranger's arm hung over my shoulder while he sagged like a sack of rice. Chang-wei held on to the other side as we dragged him through the narrow lane.

"I don't know." Chang-wei breathed heavily. "I think I was supposed to meet him."

"He's Japanese."

"I believe so."

I was still angry with him. More so now that we had an unconscious stranger propped between us. The man wasn't nearly as big as I'd first imagined him, but he was still heavy.

I shifted the dead weight onto my shoulder. "He carries a sword."

"I noticed."

"*Two.*"

We had removed the sword belt, and Chang-wei had the weapons slung over his shoulder as we made our slow progress. Though the stranger was dressed as a commoner, his swords told a different story. Captain Zhao had made it clear to us that among the Japanese, commoners weren't allowed to carry such weapons. Certainly no one in the Chinese quarter was allowed to be armed.

"Why couldn't you just tell me what you were planning?" I demanded.

"You would insist on coming along." Now he was the one frustrated. "I didn't have time to argue."

"So you tried to *drug* me?"

"I only intended for you to sleep soundly through the night. Zhao would have seen to you once you awoke."

I made an impatient sound. I knew what would come next: *Soling, it's too dangerous.* Headman Aguda didn't send me on this mission because I was meek or incapable of defending myself. I started to point that out but stopped when I recalled the real reason I was assigned. Aguda wanted me to act as his informant. Even though the two of us were friends, that was enough to keep Chang-wei from trusting me.

Fortunately, the *karakuri* teahouse wasn't far. I was correct in assuming Chang-wei was headed there. The doorway was open, and we followed the lanterns to it. Yelu was waiting for us as we entered.

The proprietor stood as unblinking as his mechanical dolls while we lowered our burden to the floor. "You killed your guide."

His matter-of-fact tone told me a story in and of itself. Yelu was prepared for anything.

"He's not dead." Chang-wei removed the sword belt from his shoulder and dropped the swords with a thud beside the body.

"What a headache." The proprietor moved to close the door behind us before giving me the eye. "And you didn't come alone."

"Plans change." Chang-wei let out a tired breath and rubbed at his shoulder while he regarded me. "How long will he be unconscious?"

"The subjects were usually unconscious for only a few minutes."

Chang-wei gave me an odd look.

I frowned right back at him. "We had to test the formula. We carry out our own inquiries, just like the Ministry of Science."

The hollow needle had held a concentrated dose of hong zao seed and mimosa root, now injected into the stranger's bloodstream. He started to stir, shaking his head groggily. He muttered something in Japanese.

"An odd pair," Yelu concluded as he brought a cup of tea and a soaked washcloth to the fallen swordsman. "Makoto is to be your guide. If he's of any use anymore."

"He might feel a little dizzy for the next hour."

Makoto opened one eye to regard me haughtily. "Just a quick nap," he growled before reaching for his swords. He kept a sharp eye on us as he pushed onto his feet. Once upright, he wavered only the slightest bit before righting himself. I had to admit, it was an impressive show of balance. Most of the test subjects had been unable to stand without weaving.

Though the swordsman felt like a sack of rocks while draped over my shoulder, Makoto was tall and lean of build. He was long in the face, with a strong jaw roughened by a growth of stubble. He also had the darkened look of someone who spent most days out in the sun.

"So *Shina*, you wish for passage into Nagasaki?" He strapped his swords back on as he spoke. His words came out slurred, still touched by the drug. After some confusion, I realized the question was directed at Chang-wei.

"Yes, and I'm prepared to pay for the privilege."

Makoto and Chang-wei continued to stare each other down, each man assessing the other. "What are you transporting? Silk, ginseng . . . opium?"

"Only myself."

"Both of us," I corrected.

Chang-wei didn't argue, but his jaw tightened. Makoto observed the exchange between us. "Your wife?"

We both fell silent.

Makoto inspected his sleeve near his elbow where I'd pierced the cloth. He pinned a hard look on me, but I detected the faint trace of a smile on his lips. "You're good with a sewing needle."

Apparently felling a warrior, despite being underhanded about it, earned me a measure of respect. Makoto displayed no respect for Chang-wei, however.

"They cut off the hands of opium smugglers." He had a disconcerting habit of resting his hand on his sword while he spoke.

Chang-wei didn't flinch. "Then it's fortunate we have none."

"Perhaps. The only thing the shogunate finds more dangerous than opium is foreign ideas." He looked Chang-wei up and down once more. "We should go quickly, *Shina*. The guards will be at their dinner."

9

A trip to the teahouse kitchen in back revealed another secret. Yelu pulled open a trapdoor hidden beneath the crates in the corner. Makoto climbed down into the darkness, and the proprietor lowered a lantern to him.

"You can trust the swordsman," Yelu assured, turning back to face us. "He's an honorable man."

Who happened to be a smuggler?

Chang-wei nodded before lowering himself down feet first. I was the last to go. Gripping the sides of the tunnel, I met Yelu's gaze as I prepared to descend. How did we know we could trust him?

I suppose we had no choice. He was one of our countrymen, and Manchurian as well. He'd held this station since my father's time and would continue to hold it.

There was no more time to ponder. I sank below the line of the floorboards, and Yelu slid the trapdoor back in place.

Chang-wei caught me around the waist to lower me to the ground. My pulse raced as we stood close in the darkened tunnel, but I was still upset with him. Just a little.

"Follow me," Makoto directed, holding up the lantern. "The

Japanese working inside the settlement will be leaving the gates now. Any *Shina-jin* outside will be returning. The guards will be occupied."

The tunnel was tall enough for us to comfortably stand and wide enough for two of us to walk side by side. Makoto took the lead while Chang-wei and I followed.

"What would a *Shina-jin* like you want in Nagasaki? There's drink and women to be had here in the quarter."

Chang-wei refused to be baited. "We're paying for speed and no questions, Makoto-san."

The light swung away as Makoto turned to us, grinning. "Do you know the punishment for being caught outside the quarter without permission?"

"Imprisonment."

But if we were caught, the imperial court in Peking would be unable to rescue us. Or unwilling.

"Imprisonment," Makoto echoed. "But my punishment for smuggling you out would be death."

"Why risk it, then?"

"One cannot buy rice and fish with air," the swordsman replied with a shrug. He turned back around, guiding us forward.

Money was Makoto's answer, but what was Chang-wei's? The lantern cast his face into deep shadow. "Why did you have to do this? Captain Zhao was already arranging something for you."

"We don't have time, Soling," he said beneath his breath. "I don't have time."

"Who is it you're looking for?" Makoto asked. The light disappeared momentarily around a corner as Makoto moved out of sight. We scrambled to follow after it.

"A man by the name of Sagara Shintarō," Chang-wei replied. "Do you know of him?"

He didn't. "Do you know how to find this man?"

"Once we're aboveground, I'll know how to find him."

Chang-wei seemed confident despite this being his first time in Nagasaki.

The tunnel turned once and then again. Makoto stopped us, motioning for us to remain quiet. "Keep moving straight ahead. Feel your way along the wall and follow my footsteps."

Without further warning, he extinguished the lantern. I bit back a gasp as blackness surrounded us. Desperately, I reached out to Chang-wei, grasping at his arm. He closed his hand around mine and squeezed.

My pulse raced as I waved a hand blindly in front of my face. I could hear Makoto's footsteps retreating, leaving us.

"Keep going forward." Chang-wei's voice came to me in the darkness. I wanted to say I felt safe as long as I was with Chang-wei, but it wasn't true. We had survived many such adventures together in the past, but the Chang-wei beside me was more stubborn and more reckless than before.

And he was keeping even more secrets from me than before.

I stumbled forward as instructed, praying we'd find our way out soon.

I LOST all sense of direction in the darkness. If Makoto were to leave us here, we'd be lost and stranded. I forced myself to take a breath, pushing back the rising panic.

"Everything will be fine," Chang-wei assured.

"I'm all right," I said, unable to keep my voice from shaking.

I didn't want Chang-wei to think he had to worry about me.

Makoto was once again before us. I heard the sound of something heavy being dragged over the dirt floor. A sliver of light filtered into the tunnel, but it was enough to guide us to a small passage. Chang-wei crawled through first, and I followed on my hands and knees.

As we straightened, Makoto reignited his lantern. We were in a cellar filled with large barrels and earthenware jars.

"There are clothes in the chest in the corner," Makoto instructed as he shoved a wooden cask over the opening.

Chang-wei and I picked through the pile of clothing. I selected a dark-colored cotton robe and turned away to dress. Though I'd chosen the smallest garment there, it still hung loosely around me as I tied the belt around my waist.

"I don't smuggle many women through this tunnel," Makoto remarked as he looked over the men's clothing on me.

A boy would attract less notice anyway, but hopefully we wouldn't be seen at all.

"Will the streets be empty?" Chang-wei asked. His gray kimono fit better than mine.

Makoto went to peer out the window. "Nagasaki is a night city. Teahouses, theater, brothels. This distillery lies on the edge of it. Once we're outside the city borders, there are open fields."

"There's a peak overlooking the harbor in the surrounding hills. The one with a tower," Chang-wei said.

"Ghost Hill." Makoto's frown deepened. "They say birds won't fly there. Strange lights can sometimes be seen over it at night."

Chang-wei's expression remained unreadable. "That's the place."

"How do you know of it?" I asked. He'd only been in the city as long as I had.

"Remember the signal tower in Peking?"

The one that had received the coded signals. "You were searching for a tower from the airship," I said.

"It stood to reason its counterpart would be built upon a high point around Nagasaki Bay."

Makoto frowned. "What is this talk of signals? Communication with foreigners is strictly forbidden by the shogunate."

"So where does your loyalty to the shogunate stand?" Chang-wei asked quietly.

They were two wolves, quietly circling each other.

"I'm only loyal to the twin gods of gold and silver."

"But you're samurai." Chang-wei's gaze dropped to the swords at his side.

Makoto dragged the edge of his cloak over the weapons. "I was once samurai. That is all you need to know."

WE CLIMBED the stairs up to the empty distillery floor. The room was dark, though light filtered in from the street outside. I could make out the outline of several large vats. Pipes formed a maze between them, and we wove around the machinery as we followed Makoto. The scent of fermented barley filled the air.

"Shōchū," he explained. "Good quality."

Despite the darkness, Makoto moved with ease. At the door, he stopped and turned to us.

"There is a magic lantern play at the Kabuki theater house tonight. Most of the night city will be gathered there. If we encounter anyone, keep your heads down and say nothing. Now stay close."

The door opened to cool night air. Sounds of the Nagasaki nightlife filtered through the streets. A startled cry rose, presumably from the theater crowd, and I was hungry to find out more about this magic lantern, but we had no time to explore.

The underground passage had taken us far from the walls of the Chinese quarter. The buildings rose two or three stories high and were packed closely together. We moved along the empty streets as quietly as we could, using only the light of the moon to guide our way.

Gradually, the sounds of the city faded behind us. More than an hour passed in silence, with me putting one foot in front of the other and wondering about the man who'd been enlisted as our guide as well as the nature of our mission.

When we reached the fields, Makoto adjusted a panel over his lantern, narrowing the light down to a single beam. It emitted a thin ray to illuminate the way ahead of us but shielded the rest of the lantern from sight. My wooden sandals sunk into the soft earth as we followed through the fields. Crops grew in rows on either side of us.

"Who is this Sagara Shintarō?" Makoto asked finally, breaking the chain of silence.

"A scientist and an inventor. Our chief engineer met with him many years ago. I wish to speak with him."

"Seems like a lot of trouble for a conversation."

"As you said, Makoto-san, ideas can be powerful."

"Dangerous. I said that ideas were dangerous," Makoto corrected. "Which is why the flow of foreign books and writings into our domain is strictly regulated."

"What is it you usually smuggle?" I asked.

Makoto glanced over his shoulder. I couldn't see his expression clearly in the dark, but he answered readily enough. "Silk. Porcelain. Whatever there is a taste for in Nagasaki. Taxes on foreign shipments make Chinese goods two or three times more expensive. Some merchants prefer to bypass the port authorities."

"Do you ever transport opium?" I had to know.

The swordsman stopped so abruptly, I almost collided with his back. I was close enough now to see the cold look on his face. "If I had discovered you were smuggling that filth, I would have left you in the tunnels to rot."

He bowed to me as he delivered the threat, the polite gesture making his warning all the more dire. From what I knew of samurai, they did not lie. And certainly not when it came to killing.

"Good," I replied, my voice grating in my throat. Despite my fear, I held my gaze steady, though I had to tilt my chin upward to meet his eyes. "Then I know we can trust you."

"Why is that, *Shina*?" he challenged.

"Because there are things you won't do for money."

10

W e walked for hours through the surrounding fields with only brief stops for rest. Before dawn, we had reached the foot of the hills and were preparing to begin our climb. I was winded, and a blister was forming on both feet from the ill-fitting sandals.

"Let us rest for a moment," Chang-wei said after seeing how I struggled.

I gave him a grateful look. I didn't want to complain or hold the group back, but I needed to catch my breath. Life in the Forbidden City had made me soft.

We rested on some stones while Makoto passed around a gourd of water. I took a swallow, but it did little to refresh me.

"You have an interesting choice of bodyguards," Makoto remarked, looking from Chang-wei to me.

"No choice at all, really," Chang-wei replied dryly.

I wasn't too tired to shoot him a glare, which he either didn't see or ignored.

Thankfully, we only climbed partway up the trail a short distance before Makoto declared we were safe to rest. We settled down on a crag of rock hidden by the surrounding brush.

Though it was out in the open and on cold, hard stone, I curled up in my cloak and fell asleep the moment my eyes were closed.

When I awoke, the area was awash in the gray light of morning. Chang-wei was asleep with his face turned toward me, eyes closed. His hand had come to rest close to mine. As if he were reaching for me in the night.

It may have been wishful thinking, but I brushed my hand over his, needing the contact, no matter how brief. Chang-wei had artists' fingers. Long and well formed.

A shadow fell over us, and Chang-wei started awake. I withdrew and stared up at Makoto.

"Time to go."

With little to pack or prepare, we simply picked ourselves up and brushed the dirt from our clothes before resuming our climb. We stuffed cold rice cakes with red bean into our mouths without stopping to eat. Makoto seemed to need no sustenance or rest at all. He pushed on relentlessly, his long legs conquering the trail much more easily than my shorter ones.

I was so focused on the climb that it took me a while to notice what was wrong. The hillside was eerily silent, absent of birdsong, just as Makoto had described. A shiver ran down my spine, and my skin prickled.

Ghost Hill. The Japanese certainly tended toward the dramatic.

Chang-wei drew closer and held out his hand. Cradled in his palm was a rosewood box with a compass inside. The needle spun erratically from one pole to another. Some invisible force was affecting the lodestone.

Finally the tower appeared in the distance. Compared to the graceful shrines that dotted hillsides, this structure was a monstrosity. The steel gray frame blended into the dark rock of the surrounding cliffs. It was very easy to overlook unless one knew it was there.

As we neared the top of the ridge, the structure loomed large overhead. It resembled a skeletal pagoda, with all that was graceful and sacred gutted out. A faint hum vibrated the air, like the buzz of insects. An unnatural presence seemed to hover around us.

The base of the tower separated out into four legs. A shelter had been built beside it, and long wires extended down from the metal latticework into the roof of the building.

The signal tower was clearly abandoned. A layer of rust clung to the iron, and moss crept over the adjoining building.

"A control station," Chang-wei declared as he moved steadily toward it.

Makoto hung back just as a thin ribbon of lightning snapped across the latticework. Chang-wei was undaunted by the phenomenon. He was close enough to peer into the windows of the control station where the paper panes had disintegrated.

I went to stand beside Chang-wei. Inside, the station was indeed abandoned. Instead of a human operator, there was a contraption built of steel and wire. A series of wheels churned out a pattern, which was transmitted to a mechanical wand that tapped rhythmically against the signal generator.

Chang-wei exhaled as he stared at the contraption. It was a simple automaton, built to repeatedly tap out a message. Hope drained out of him.

"This is Sagara Shintarō's work," he insisted, jaw tight. "We have to find him."

I tried to reassure him, despite my doubts. "We'll find a way."

I watched the mechanical finger tap out another message before the cycle began to repeat.

A loud click broke through the trance. I swung around to see a young woman at the edge of clearing. She had a rifle propped against her shoulder and aimed squarely at us. When Makoto drew his sword, the woman swung the weapon toward him instead.

She barked a command to Makoto in Japanese, I assumed for

him to drop his weapon. Unlike the women I'd seen in Nagasaki, her kimono-style top ended just above her knees, resembling a jacket rather than a robe. Beneath it she wore trousers that were closely fitted. Her sleeves were also shortened in length. The wide sash at her waist was worked in leather rather than silk, and I could see another pistol holstered at her side.

Behind her stood a samurai warrior in full armor, his face occluded with a battle mask. He held a spear in hand and looked in every way larger, stronger and more menacing than Makoto. Makoto lowered his sword but maintained his grip on it.

"We have business here with Lord Sagara Shintarō," Chang-wei declared.

The woman kept her weapon aimed. Outwardly, I forced myself to remain composed, but my heart was pounding so hard it threatened to burst.

"*Shina-jin.*" Her next words were in accented but understandable Canton dialect, often used for trade. "Sagara Shintarō is my father. He has been dead for over five years."

SAGARA SATOMI LED us to a secluded area where the hill flattened out to a plateau. A lonely wooden building stood sheltered within the trees. It appeared abandoned. Tiles were missing from the roof, and the paper windows were torn in places.

"My father's *Rangaku* school."

"Dutch learning," Chang-wei added, for my benefit. I thought of the Western astronomy book he had bought for me.

Satomi stepped through the wild grass with confidence in her stride. Her hair was braided to one side. Tied back and out of the way. She was dressed for ease of movement rather than grace or beauty. The almost mannish clothing would have been out of place in Nagasaki, but here she was in harmony with her surroundings. This was her domain.

The formidable swordsman followed closely behind her. Even without his armor and weapons, his towering height would have been enough to chase away any threat. When Satomi swung open the double doors, he entered first.

"Yoshiro will not allow me to walk into danger," she explained before beckoning us inside.

The bodyguard stood by the far wall as we entered. The main room was bare of everything except for a few tattered mats lining the floors and a scroll on the wall. The painting itself was perhaps unremarkable. Four characters in a bold strokes, the words themselves serving as art. But what set the work apart was the splatter of dark red across it.

The moment I saw the stain, my heart seized. It marked the paper as well as the wall behind it. Blood. It had to be blood, and there was nothing else decorating the walls except for this one splash of red. Violence long past, left on display like a scar.

"It was here," Satomi confirmed, her voice as hard as steel.

She turned toward the inner chamber without another word. I glanced at Chang-wei uncertainly. He was the first to follow after her.

The second chamber was a book room. The shelves were full of various volumes covered in a layer of gray dust. The air in the place was oppressive and haunted, yet my fingers still itched to open the books to peer inside.

We continued through a sliding door at the back, which led us out into what had once been a garden. The greenery was overgrown and unkempt, but at least I could breathe easy without the shadow of death that clung to the walls inside.

"Your father was a great man," Chang-wei began. "I'm sorry to hear of his passing."

A flicker of grief crossed her face but was immediately banished. We were strangers, after all. "You wanted something from him," she replied coldly. "They all do."

"My father was the head of the Ministry of Science in Peking.

Lord Sagara once considered him a colleague," I said, hoping Satomi would understand. "His life was also taken from him."

For a moment, our eyes met. We could have been mirror images, living parallel lives across the sea. Her pain was an echo of my pain.

Satomi gestured toward the abandoned building. "After the Chinese defeat, the shogunate became more wary of foreigners. The number of ships allowed through Nagasaki was reduced. Foreign goods and ideas were frowned upon. We shouldn't need them, the shogunate insisted. Many *Rangaku* schools were closed down, but this remote location stayed open. My father continued to study and experiment. Then one day, the *hitokiri* came for him."

"*Hitokiri*?"

"Assassins," Satomi explained.

"Highly skilled assassins," Makoto amended. His tone held both reverence and fear. "Four renowned killers used for special assignments by the shogunate."

"Skill wasn't necessary." Bitterness seeped into her tone. "The *hitokiri* entered the school while the pupils were at their lessons. My father took one look at him and knew he had only a moment to decide how he would die. He calmly sent us from the room and told us to shut the doors." Closing her eyes, she turned away. "I never heard a sound."

I remembered my father taking my hand as he walked through our front gate for the last time. His grasp had been steady, even though he must have known he would never return. My heart ached all over again.

Chang-wei was the first to break the silence. "This is a great loss for both our nations."

"The shogunate doesn't believe so."

"We had hoped to reestablish communications with Lord Sagara. To unite our two nations under a common purpose." He was ever the diplomat.

"You're here because you need a way to fight the English," she replied bluntly. "And my father knew their ways well."

Yoshiro the bodyguard came forward. Bending down, he pushed one of the boulders in the garden aside to reveal a shallow pit. Inside was a bundle wrapped in coarse cloth. Satomi unwrapped the stash and pulled out a rifle fashioned of wood and steel. Slender and lethal.

"Take a close look, *Shina-jin.*" Straightening, she tossed the firearm through the air at Chang-wei, who caught it in both hands. "When you're assured it meets with your approval, then name your price."

Chang-wei stared at the weapon in his hands, turning it over and over. I thought he would deny that he'd come to purchase arms, but instead a shrewd look crossed his face.

"I need to see how it fires," he said.

To his left, Makoto tensed at the sudden turn of events. I was equally surprised but had no chance to question Chang-wei.

Satomi nodded. "Come see for yourself."

Yoshiro pushed the boulder back in place and took up the rear as we exited the grounds of the school. In the open area out back, a row of painted targets had been set up. She held her hand out for the rifle.

"If you attempt to aim this at me or overpower me in any way, Yoshiro will deal with you swiftly," she warned as she loaded two iron rounds into the chamber.

"I wouldn't think of it, Lady Sagara. We *Shina-jin* are not without honor."

She handed the rifle back to him, muzzle pointed up. "Do you know how to shoot it?"

Chang-wei answered by facing the target. His expression became focused as Satomi stepped back. With the butt end set against his shoulder, Chang-wei took aim and pulled the trigger.

An explosion split the air, loud enough to rattle the wooden frame of the schoolhouse. I jumped back and collided with

Makoto, who reached out to steady me. Fifty paces away, there was a hole on the left side of the target. My ears rang.

"Not bad," Satomi remarked, coming up beside him. "Just need a little practice."

Chang-wei handed over the rifle, and she took aim much quicker, as if the weapon were an extension of herself. A second explosion rang out, the force of it sending Satomi back a step as she absorbed the recoil. The shot landed squarely in the center of the target.

"Any coward can kill a man from a hundred paces," Makoto muttered.

Satomi ignored him to direct her inquiry to Chang-wei. "So what is your offer?"

"How many do you have?" Chang-wei countered.

"This one here."

"I'll need more."

Why was he negotiating a deal to purchase arms? This wasn't what we had come for.

Satomi narrowed her eyes shrewdly and lowered the rifle. "How many more, *Shina-jin*?"

"Thousands," Chang-wei replied. "Tens of thousands. Enough to supply an army."

11

Satomi let out a sharp laugh at Chang-wei's request, while Makoto was much more direct. He reached for his sword.

"Who are you?" he demanded.

Seeing his movement, the bodyguard Yoshiro reached for his sword as well. I threw myself between Chang-wei and the Japanese swordsmen, though my weapons were useless in this standoff.

"There's no need to fight."

Chang-wei alone remained levelheaded. "I'm proposing an exchange, Lady Sagara. For the sake of our two nations."

"For a thousand guns that can be turned against us?" Makoto spat. "You're no merchant trader, *Shina*."

"It hardly matters." Satomi regarded them both, bemused. "I craft each of these weapons by hand, as my father did. I could not create a thousand of them in my lifetime."

"We don't need the guns. We need the knowledge of how to make them."

Satomi regarded him warily. "Who are you?" she asked, echoing Makoto's earlier question.

"Engineer Chen Chang-wei, of the Ministry of Science in Peking."

She looked to me. "The same Ministry your father once served."

"I serve the imperial court as well."

"The Chinese imperial court." Her mouth quirked. She looked to her bodyguard. "How important we must be, Yoshi-chan, to warrant such a visit."

The bodyguard did not appear amused. His eyes gleamed from behind his war mask, and his hand refused to relax from his sword.

"With your knowledge and expertise, we can send the foreigners from our shores," Chang-wei proposed.

Satomi smirked. "The guns are for sale; I'm not. If you are not here to buy, then we have no further business."

A muscle ticked along Chang-wei's jaw as he measured his response. "An alliance would benefit both the empires of China and Japan, Lady Sagara."

"Engineer Chen, is it?"

I considered it some progress. At least she was no longer referring to him as *Shina-jin*.

"I am no lady. To the *bakufu*, I am nothing, so it serves you no purpose to negotiate with me."

"Then who can we make an appeal to?"

She remained skeptical. "Your presence here puts me in danger. Why should I help you?"

"Because our fathers respected each other," I interjected. "Lord Sagara believed in collaboration between our nations."

Satomi regarded me for a long time. "I am not my father," she said quietly. "He was not born samurai, nor was he from a wealthy family. It was only through diligence and ingenuity that he was elevated to the rank of the samurai. He believed in learning from others, even if they were outsiders." She bowed her head in reverence.

"Seek out Karakuri Giemon," she said finally. "He may be sympathetic to your cause."

"KARAKURI GIEMON IS THE MECHANICAL WIZARD," Makoto translated for us. "He's a famous inventor who resides in the Saga domain, at least two days by foot."

Satomi had allowed us shelter temporarily before retreating into the schoolhouse. We were left to debate our next course of action.

Chang-wei looked to me. "Two days there, two days back. Every day we're away, we risk being caught."

"Do you want to go back?" I asked him.

"No, but—"

"Neither do I," I interrupted.

"If we're imprisoned by the shogunate, the imperial court won't be able to help us. One of us should return to Nagasaki."

Which meant me. "We go together or not at all."

Yelu, Lord Sagara, Satomi and even this inventor were somehow connected to my father. And to me.

"We'll go and meet this *karakuri* master," I said, daring Chang-wei to object. "If Makoto-san will take us."

Our gazes locked, and I could see the arguments brewing beneath Chang-wei's cool demeanor. Eventually he said nothing.

Small victory.

Makoto listened to our conversation with great interest. "As long as your silver is good," he replied, but there was something hidden beneath his casual tone. "And one small request."

"What request?" Chang-wei turned away from our battle of wills.

"Once my part of the bargain is done," Makoto dismissed.

He descended back down to Nagasaki to prepare for the

journey while we stayed hidden and explored the *Rangaku* school.

The building had been left as it was when Lord Sagara was assassinated. Tools remained on the benches inside a workroom. A wooden box painted with a cloud and lightning design sat gathering dust in the corner. Twin coils of wire rose from it, and there was a wheel attached at the base with a foot pedal. Chang-wei pushed the lid back, and we both peered at smaller wheel structure inside.

"An *elekiteru*," Chang-wei observed. "I wonder if it's operational."

There was some resemblance to the device we had found in my father's Japanese puzzle box, though on a larger scale. Chang-wei seated himself at the foot pedals. With some creaking, the wheel started to turn. I waited, watching with anticipation, but nothing happened.

"Maybe I can get it working again."

"Have you ever seen one of these before?" I asked him.

Chang-wei was undaunted as he removed the lid. "What one man can do, so can another."

From his absorbed expression, I knew he would be in another world for the next few hours.

I wandered to a yellowed volume left on the shelf and flipped through it. One of the prints showed a man in Western clothing, flying a kite with lightning flashing in the background.

"This is interesting." I held up the book to Chang-wei, who only spared it a cursory glance before returning to the *elekiteru*.

"He's a famous scientist from *Měiguó*," Chang-wei said dismissively. "He lived a hundred years ago."

Měiguó. The beautiful country on the other side of the world. America, they called it. I had met a merchant from this place once. Dean Burton had been an associate of Chang-wei's. Mister Burton was fair skinned with yellow hair and eyes that were disconcertingly blue. This scientist had been drawn with similarly pale hair. A key hung cryptically from the end of a long kite string. I pondered that for a moment before turning the page.

Reading Japanese script presented an endless puzzle. Some of the characters were similar to Chinese ones, but other than a few words here and there, I couldn't make sense of it. The pictures themselves told a story of mysterious devices and wires and energy flowing between them.

"There is a branch of study using electricity to treat illness," Chang-wei commented from the corner. His arms disappeared into the wooden box as the tinkered with the device. "They believe *elekiteru* can be used to stimulate the organs."

"Like our concept of qi," I suggested. "Our medical practices are based on redirecting internal energy to specific points to stimulate organs and promote balance and healing."

"It's possible. I haven't given it much thought."

Chang-wei's quick dismissal stung. I frowned at him, but he was too immersed in his machine to notice.

"Electricity comes from lightning," he explained. "It can also be generated through motion and travels along copper wire."

"Qi is generated through breath and meditation," I argued. "And travels along nerves and blood vessels. Doesn't that sound similar?"

"Symbolism can be found anywhere, Soling. It's for poetry, not science. When one looks carefully, much of what we consider learning is merely based on symbolism. Yin and yang, light and dark. Balance."

Chang-wei worked the pedals, and the wheel inside whirred to life, spinning for a time before gradually winding down. From his dark scowl, I assumed this latest effort was unsuccessful.

"What is wrong with yin and yang and balance? These forces are universal."

"They *feel* right to you. Because you look around yourself and you see men and women and light and darkness, so it's easy to see the world in such opposing contrasts. But other than the sense of comfort it gives you, how quantifiable is it?"

My skin prickled at his use of *you*. As if this were my own personal ignorance.

"I'm not saying there are not remedies that, for reasons unknown, are effective," Chang-wei continued. "But how often are they effective? Why does acupuncture sometimes cure a man and sometimes do nothing?"

"Because everyone's energy flow and imbalances are different."

"Ah, see?" Chang-wei looked up then, triumphant. "Qi defies measurement. How do I know if something inside me is due to an imbalance of qi or simply indigestion because I ate spoiled meat?"

I was ready to throw my book at him, but I didn't want to damage the book. "You seem to imply that Western learning is better than ours. While our findings are merely based on symbols and poetry."

Chang-wei must have detected the sharp edge in my tone. His argument became more formal, academic, as if debating his colleagues in the Ministry. "From what I can see, Western learning is based on measurement. Definitive rules and observations."

"What about cutting into a body that's already sick?" I challenged. "Bleeding out bad humors? Destroying the body to heal it? Is that measurable?"

He raised his eyebrows in surprise.

"We mystics in the Court of Physicians aren't completely ignorant. When we're not reading tea leaves, we do read a book or two." I laid the book open on the lid of the *elekiteru* before turning on my heel. "There's a diagram of your precious box."

I left him to his tinkering. It was the first time Chang-wei and I had clashed like that. On the surface, it might have sounded like a scientific debate, but my chest was tight, my throat constricted with anger.

At the heart of his logic, something else seemed to lurk. The insinuation that Western thinking was not merely different but somehow superior to Chinese beliefs.

Many whispered that Chen Chang-wei was a Western sympathizer, which was a more polite way of insinuating that he was a traitor. In thought if not in action. Could someone who thought Western thinking was superior still remain loyal to the empire? Emperor Yizhu hated the *Yangguizi* and everything that had to do with the West.

I didn't know the answer, but Chang-wei's attitude didn't sit well with me. I knew he was inventive and open to new ideas. The way his mind worked left me confounded. Much like how my brother could break anything down to its parts, and from the pieces its essence. The soul of it and what made it work.

But Chang-wei's talk of mysticism, symbolism and yin and yang left a bitter taste in my mouth.

I wandered to the rooms toward the back of the courtyard, our argument hanging over me like a black cloud. My logic wasn't as precise and clear-cut as Chang-wei's, but what came to my mind was the memory of the first time I had tried to measure someone's pulse.

"What am I looking for?" I had asked Physician Lo.

The old man shook his head. "Just feel. Observe."

So I felt for the patient's pulse. I noted the strength of it, the rhythm of each beat. And then I did the same for another patient. And another. Some who were sick and most who were well. Over days and weeks and months, I learned the heart rhythms of the villagers we served. Learning whose pulse might skip, gauging what sort of conditions would cause an irregular or weakened pulse.

Chang-wei might call it meditation or mysticism, but I began to get a sense of a person's individual energy. His wellness. His qi.

Qi wasn't pulse. Or breath. Or heat. Or the beat of one's heart. It was all those things, together. Immeasurable, but not unknowable.

I'd reached what looked like a sleeping room. It was a long chamber lined with a single mat. A layer of dust clung to the floor, and cobwebs hung in the corners. During its time, the school had space enough to house fifteen to twenty students. The disciples would have slept here in the communal room, then awoken to prepare for lessons in the main room.

But this thriving environment was ended by a single assassin's blade.

I couldn't ignore the similarities between my father's death and Lord Sagara's. Both were men of science and engineering. They were scholars more than politicians, yet they'd been executed for treason when their countries needed them most.

I left the sleeping quarters to go to the rear of the compound. A building made of stone and brick stood apart from the other chambers. Satomi's bodyguard stood at the door. As I neared, he moved to block my path.

"Yoshiro, let her pass," came the command from inside.

The warrior's black eyes peered at me from behind his mask, but finally he stepped aside. My shoulders tensed as I moved past him. His steely gaze followed my every move.

Inside, Satomi stood at a workbench with a pistol in one hand and a hammer in the other. Around the shop were metal and wooden parts. At first I said nothing, content to just watch as she worked. Satomi tapped iron pins in place on the stock, her movements practiced and efficient.

"My father taught me," she said between hammer strikes. "He was interested in the making of firearms using techniques that he learned from the Westerners."

She continued assembling the weapon as I ventured closer. "My younger brother is like you."

"Oh?" Satomi raised an eyebrow while her focus remained on the work in front of her.

"He has a talent for knowing how parts should fit together to make a working whole. And for making new creations."

"No talent here, Miss Jin. I just repeat what my father did before me. Over and over until the knowledge sinks into my bones."

Satomi paused to wipe her brow, and I looked to the diagrams tacked onto the walls. Some were old and worn, but many were newly drawn.

"You took over your father's trade after his death?" I asked.

"This wasn't his trade. My father was a scholar. A statesman."

"A samurai?"

She looked up sharply at my question, then nodded. "Yes. Samurai."

Lord Sagara was well respected, which is why my father had made contact with him. The two had likely exchanged ideas, traded knowledge. It must have seemed like the dawning of a new age of discovery—yet shortly after my father had left this world, Lord Sagara was soon to follow.

"These weapons you make. I can't see how they're not of great value to your empire."

"There was a time when guns were highly prized." Satomi lifted the pistol to look down the barrel, as if sighting a target. "The warlords equipped their armies with firearms, and battles were fierce. But once those territorial wars were settled, once the Tokugawa reigned supreme, and peace came to our land, such weapons were not as necessary."

"But that's a good thing, is it not?"

"Peace is a good thing," Satomi agreed soberly. Setting down the pistol, she reached for a sander and began to file down the edge of the stock. "My father was a scientist. He loved knowledge for knowledge's sake. I imagine yours was the same."

"He was." I came closer so only the workbench separated us. My throat tightened hearing her speak of her father and of mine in the same breath. We were still strangers to each other, yet sisters in spirit.

"My father was also practical," she continued. "He knew the Western armies continued to use firearms, and that their weapons and ships were growing more powerful. Yet the *bakufu*—"

"*Bakufu?*"

"Our government," she explained. "The shogunate. The feudal lords were insistent that we had protected ourselves by closing our borders. With peace within and foreign influences kept out, it was easy to be lulled into a sense of security. We didn't need the brutality of firearms. Perhaps that is true, but my father continued to study them, and continued to study Western sciences as well."

"And the shogunate didn't approve of his studies." I imagined a country that would shut out all foreigners must have been similarly wary of foreign ideas. Our empire was no different.

"The *bakufu* values tradition and the ways of the samurai, which have become legendary. There is a romance to it, the rule of the sword and the samurai code of honor. There is no romance to the way a firearm kills."

Absently, she ran her fingers along the stock of the weapon, feeling each curve. Satisfied, she reached for an oiled rag and began to polish the metal. "You haven't asked why my father was assassinated."

"It is not my place to ask."

"But you want to know." Satomi set the pistol down and the rag beside it. She braced her hands against the workbench and drew in a deep breath.

"I want to know because I have questions of my own," I admitted.

"We have tradition here called *katakiuchi*. Legal vendetta. One can petition for vendetta on behalf of someone who has suffered a wrongful death. Once *katakiuchi* is invoked against someone, his life is forfeit. He can be pursued openly and killed in broad daylight without fearing repercussion." Satomi looked directly at me, her jaw set in a hard line. "There was a dispute, and one of my father's rifles was used to kill a ranking samurai. A sword maker is not held responsible for the lives his blades might take. But in the case of a firearm, the traditionalists believe, since there was so little skill required to pull the trigger, that the death was in part caused by the maker. But the truth is there is a faction within the *bakufu* that hates foreigners. My father was outspoken in defending outsiders and foreign ideas, so he had to die. It was a pointless death."

She bit off the last words as fire flashed in her eyes. This was a wound that hadn't healed. I felt the echo of my own wound deep in my chest.

"My father was killed for declaring the Western forces superior to ours," I told her.

"When my father was put to death, many thought I would take my own life and follow him. Cleaner for everyone involved that way. But I didn't," Satomi declared defiantly.

"We were destitute," I commiserated. "It was thought that my mother and I would have to sell ourselves into servitude, yet no one came forward to help us."

It was strange to be speaking so openly to a stranger, and a foreigner at that. But the smallest crack showed in Satomi's hard exterior. "But I am not dead, and you are not a prostitute."

"There was a time I wanted to disappear. I wanted to withdraw from everything. From Peking and its politics. From this war with the *Yangguizi*. Anything to keep my family safe. But now I realize this fight is the only way to ensure our future."

I let the words sink in. It wasn't until I spoke them out loud that I realized I truly believed it. Emperor Yizhu was flawed, a young man pulled in many directions. And our empire was fighting for survival. I was part of that struggle now.

"My father used to believe that Western science applied with Eastern ethics would prevail. They called such thinking treason," Satomi recounted sadly. She picked up the pistol and held it before her in both hands. "Engineer Chen. He thinks the same way, doesn't he?"

"He was my father's pupil."

"And what is he to you?"

The bluntness of her question took me aback. Even worse, I didn't have an answer. "He's . . . he's a friend," I replied, feeling tongue-tied.

"A good enough friend to risk your life for?"

"Our empire is worth the risk."

"The empire that put your own father to death?" Her eyebrow raised once more, aiming the question like a knife at my heart.

"Yes." A sharp pain struck me as I said it. Perhaps that pain would never go away.

Satomi measured the weight behind that one word. "Here," she said finally. "This is for you."

She held out the pistol to me, and I reluctantly took it in my hands. It was heavy, yet sleek in appearance. The barrel was shorter than the length of my palm, and the metal was etched with an elegant design. It was a weapon that could easily be hidden within the fold of a sleeve or beneath a broad sash. Beautiful, despite its deadly purpose.

"I'll teach you how to use it. You'll need protection for your journey." The corner of her mouth lifted in not quite a smile. "And I'll accompany you tomorrow, if you'll permit it. You might need me as well."

12

Makoto was waiting for us at the foot of the mountain early the next day. He had secured a wagon and a team of mules, and by midmorning, we were trudging along a dirt road headed east. Yoshiro sat up front beside Makoto, who took the reins. Chang-wei and I tucked ourselves in back with Satomi.

"Hard to pass ourselves off as peasant farmers with an armed warrior guarding us," Makoto said dryly.

Yoshiro turned in his direction but said nothing. He wore his suit of armor and mask as always and conducted himself with the same rigid silence that I was coming to associate with the samurai class.

"I'm well-known among these parts," Satomi insisted. "There's no use in hiding."

"We'll be taking a less-traveled route. If we come across any patrols, the two of you remain quiet." Makoto directed a look at Chang-wei and me. "I'll do the talking."

The area we traveled did appear secluded. There were no other wagons or travelers on the dirt road.

"Is there danger out here from bandits?" Chang-wei asked.

"This domain is very secure, the roads and cities well protected. No honest work for mercenaries," Makoto said with a laugh. "Which is why I'm forced to find work among the *Shina-jin*."

The mule team fell into an easy pace. The surrounding hillsides were green and lush, and occasionally we passed through patches of farmland. I saw a few farmhands working the fields, but they paid us little attention, and we were left to our journey unmolested.

"I meant no insult, what I said yesterday," Chang-wei said to me in the middle of a long stretch of silence. His voice was lowered, meant for me alone. "I respect what you do."

"But you think it's all folk remedies and old superstitions," I countered.

He sighed. "I never said that, Soling."

Maybe I did want to pick a fight. We had gone to sleep last night barely speaking to each other. I told myself it was because Chang-wei had been absorbed in his new project with the *elekiteru*. He never did get the thing working.

"It's just frustrating sometimes. Hearing educated men speak of elixirs of immortality and forbidden points. Feeling my pulse and telling me my disposition based on every tick."

I glanced at him from the corner of my eye. "Give me your arm."

He looked at me warily.

"Your arm," I insisted with a curt nod.

Chang-wei let out a long-suffering sigh and folded back his sleeve, exposing his forearm. With a roll of his eyes, he held it out to me.

I bit back a smile. His display was somewhat endearing. He glanced over at me as I took hold of his wrist. The muscles of his arm flexed as I placed two fingers over his pulse point.

"The patient is irritable. Imbalanced," I diagnosed. "An excess of male pride."

I caught a smile from Satomi before she averted her gaze to the hillside.

"Is that so?" Chang-wei asked haughtily.

I switched to the pulse at his neck, just below his jaw. When he tilted his head upward to look at me, my own pulse jumped. When he was this close, it was impossible to deny how handsome I found him. How I was teasing him now just as an excuse to touch him.

"Definitely too much yang," I continued, my breath thin. "Prey to mood swings."

His throat moved as he swallowed. "And the cure?"

My gaze latched onto his mouth. It was finely shaped. Stubborn at times, but also clever and expressive. He often showed so little emotion that I'd learned to read his mood from the tiny quirks of his mouth. At that moment, I really wished we were alone.

"A good knock to the head," I prescribed.

He gave a short laugh, and my chest warmed. As my fingers slipped away from his neck, a thread of unease wormed its way into me. I had only been playing, not truly reading Chang-wei's condition, but for one second, I had sensed something strange. A skip in his pulse that seemed out of place.

"Soling?" he asked when I remained silent for too long.

I willed my shoulders to relax as I leaned back in the wagon beside him. "You're forgiven."

"How gracious."

I nudged him with my foot. It was childish of me, but I hadn't felt young and childish in a long time. His foot stayed close to mine, stroking a line against the arch of my slipper before falling away.

I was probably making too much of the gesture, but maybe I wasn't.

∽

WE MADE it through the first day uneventfully and set camp as the sun started to set. Makoto unhitched the mules to feed and water them while I rummaged through the supplies. There was millet and rice and a few jugs of wine.

As I gathered water from a nearby stream for the evening rice, I took a moment to look over the land. I was in a strange land with different customs and laws. Yet here, among the tall grass with the sunset painting the sky, I could have been back in our village, at the end of a long day bringing remedies to the farmers who lived out in the fields. There wasn't a quiet place like this in Peking. There was always noise from the street, from the city drums, from the temple gong signaling the hours.

I finished filling the iron pot with water and returned to camp to start the rice. At the edge of camp, Satomi sat with her bodyguard. He was turned away from me, but for once he had his helmet off. His head remained bent as she knelt beside him with her hand against his chest.

The tenderness of the moment made me uncomfortable. It was a private exchange, not meant for prying eyes. I forced my gaze away and saw Makoto, who'd come to stand beside me.

"Lady Sagara's bodyguard is *rōnin*," Makoto said.

"What does that mean?"

"He's been cast adrift. When Lord Sagara was killed, his retainers immediately became masterless, prohibited from swearing loyalty to a new lord. The others likely drifted away to find work as hired swords, but this one stayed."

"She treats him as more than a servant." I glanced back to see Satomi placing Yoshiro's helmet back on while he remained on one knee before her.

"They're both outcasts." There was no condemnation in his tone.

"Are you *rōnin* as well?"

The corner of his mouth twitched. "Plenty of us no-good drifters about."

I started to ask him about the favor he wanted from us, but Makoto was already gone, moving to get supplies from the wagon. I returned my attention to the rice.

Chang-wei knelt to start the cooking fire, and I positioned the rice pot over it. Together we sat back.

"Did you ever imagine we would travel the world together?" Chang-wei was looking in the distance. I followed his gaze to the orange glow that surrounded the hills. My breath caught at the flood of color. At the beauty of this particular moment in time, knowing it would soon be gone.

"We haven't traveled so far," I remarked. "The island empire and ours are close neighbors."

He smiled faintly. "Perhaps we'll journey farther next time."

It was rare to find Chang-wei in such a whimsical mood. He was always so serious.

"All the way to Bangkok," I suggested, drawing from the first name that came to mind.

"I would like to show you London one day."

"London?" I stiffened. "Why would I ever want to go there?"

"It's a great city, Soling. Grandiose in its own way."

I grew quiet. "We're at war with the *Yingguoren*."

"That doesn't mean I hate everything British."

"Don't you remember how they imprisoned you? They forced you to serve on their ships?"

"But I learned so many things," he countered. "Saw a place and people and wonders I never knew existed. We want to be rid of them, but the world has changed. The steamships won't disappear. The *Yingguoren* won't go away."

He seemed so earnest. Chang-wei really did believe he could embrace Western ideas while fighting against the invasion.

"You know there are those in the imperial court who hear the way you speak and doubt your loyalty, Chang-wei."

"But you don't doubt it, do you?"

I met his gaze, my heart aching. No one was more loyal to the empire than Chang-wei, but I knew the most loyal and dedicated of men could still be executed for treason. Imperial loyalty required a degree of forced blindness. Or at least silence.

"I suspect Headman Aguda may have had a motive for putting me on this mission," I confessed.

Chang-wei's expression became blank. "To report on me."

"I wouldn't do that. We're friends."

"We're more than friends."

The quiet certainty in his reply made my pulse skip. This was more than we typically admitted to each other. I could feel my skin warming under his gaze.

If he meant to say anything more, he didn't have the chance. Makoto had returned from the wagon with a jug in hand. Chang-wei moved to the cooking fire to check the rice, and I was left to wonder and fret.

I should have said something back to him. Something clever or heartfelt, instead of sitting there with my tongue frozen.

By the time Makoto seated himself, Satomi had come to join us as well. Yoshiro remained at the perimeter to keep watch. He was always vigilant.

"We'll be in Saga domain the day after next," she said, unslinging the rifle from her shoulder to set it beside her in the grass. "Takeda Hideyori will be surprised to see representatives from the *Shina* imperial court at his gate."

"Is Lord Takeda sympathetic to foreigners?" Chang-wei asked.

"Takeda-sama is a man of science," Satomi replied. "I am confident he'll welcome your arrival. He also has a special interest in foreign studies. After my father left us, Takeda-sama became my guardian."

Yet now she was out in Nagasaki alone with only one body-guard, haunting her father's domain like a ghost. Sometimes I felt that way in Peking, traveling down the corridors of the Forbidden City as my father had done.

"Why is Lord Takeda known as Karakuri Giemon?" I asked.

It was the same word the proprietor had used at the teahouse with the puppets.

"*Karakuri* is mechanical trickery," Satomi explained. "Takeda-sama's automatons are known throughout Edo."

We ate our rice mixed with dried fish and pickled radishes. Simple fare, but filling enough. Makoto poured the contents of his jug into several cups.

"Shōchū," he told me as I sniffed at the clear liquid.

I imagined it was from the same distillery we had tunneled into to sneak out of the Chinese quarter. Makoto raised his cup to make a toast.

"*Kanpai!*"

We echoed the sentiment, which happened to be one of the phrases that translated easily between the two languages.

I took a tentative sip and found the fermented taste sharper than wine but not unpleasant. Chang-wei had already drained his cup in proper fashion. A glance to the edge of the camp revealed Yoshiro in silhouette as he leaned against a tree, peering vigilantly out into the darkness. I considered extending an invitation for him to join us, but the former samurai appeared to follow a strict code of conduct. On top of that, he intimidated me with his plated armor and face shield. His eyes constantly watched us from behind the mask.

Makoto, however, cast off all sense of formality. "Everyone is still alive," he concluded, refilling his cup and raising it for another toast. "This is a good day."

～

THAT NIGHT, Satomi and I retired to the back of the wagon while the men made their beds on the ground beside it. For propriety's sake.

"I should tell you something, Soling-san," Satomi said, the

moment I found a comfortable spot among the supplies. I had one of the sacks of grain as a pillow.

I couldn't see her on the other side of the wagon, since we'd extinguished the fire to avoid alerting any wandering patrols.

"What is it?"

"When we reach Takeda-sama's house, it may be an uncomfortable situation, one I must apologize for."

"There's no need to apologize for anything."

"There is. I ran away from Takeda-sama's household three years ago. I didn't want to owe him any more than I did. You shouldn't be dragged into such personal matters."

I understood completely. "You didn't want to be a burden."

"I also left because it was assumed he would one day take me as his wife."

"Oh..."

"Not that there was any sort of scandal, though all of Takeda-sama's acquaintances assumed I was his mistress already. I was too old to be a foster daughter, and, though he was old enough to be my father, Takeda-sama was unmarried. After a year under his roof, he did ask me to be his wife. I don't know if it was out of obligation or because of the rumors, but I left the next morning."

"Just left?"

"Without a word of farewell."

And without remorse as well, it seemed.

"Was he cruel to you?"

"No, Takeda-sama was always kind."

"Then why?"

"So I wouldn't have to suffer the awkwardness of having to reply."

I bit back a laugh and heard Satomi chuckling softly in the darkness.

"He had the look of one hunted when he came to ask for me," she protested. "I couldn't subject him to such torture." Her tone became more serious. "I think being alone suits me. Or at least it suited me at the time. Yoshiro is my constant companion, but he's unable to speak."

So her bodyguard was mute. I wasn't surprised to hear of it, considering how he'd said nothing from the moment he joined our party.

"I haven't spoken with Takeda-sama since," she told me. "But I don't believe he holds a grudge. He sends people once in a while to see that I'm still alive and well. They always come and go quietly, leaving me to my life in the hills."

I had to admire her independent spirit. Satomi was so comfortable in her skin.

"How did you begin selling the firearms?" I asked her.

"My father was known for them but only sold them to wealthy collectors. He would gift them to the shogun and high-ranking lords. It gained him a buffer for a long time. Members of the *bakufu* argued that with his level of craftsmanship, his creations were more art than weaponry."

"But then he fell out of favor," I said. Satomi's story felt so achingly familiar.

"Father realized the collectors never intended for the firearms to be used. No matter how much they admired his workmanship, the *bakufu* would never support developing guns. It went against the samurai code of honor that had only strengthened over three hundred years in isolation. So Father started selling them to merchants and sailors who were not warriors. Who needed the weapons for protection."

"Your father wanted his work to have purpose."

"He wasn't an artist. He was an engineer. I first learned this trade by observing him. Bringing tea to his workshop. Lingering to watch. When it was apparent he would have no more sons, my father started to train me."

No *more* sons. I didn't miss that nuance. Had Lord Sagara's sons died?

"Then one day, the choice came to me—an honorable

marriage to Takeda Hideyori or a life of freedom, owing no one anything, using skills passed down by my ancestors. The answer was clear."

"Chang-wei and I were also once intended to be married," I confessed. I'm not sure why I revealed it then—perhaps I felt I owed her something for being so direct with me.

"Ah, that explains it."

"Explains what?" I asked.

I could hear her shifting in the darkness, trying to find a more comfortable position. "All the long glances," she said with a laugh. "And the brooding looks."

I wanted to demand *whose* long glances and *whose* brooding looks she spoke of, but I decided, very wisely, to remain quiet. Chang-wei and I were no longer held together by any promises or agreements. There were times I thought and wondered whether it was possible. Whether *we* were possible. Sometimes late at night when I was alone in bed. Or when we were together, talking of anything and nothing.

After returning to Peking, Chang-wei never mentioned anything between us. He never spoke of how we'd faced death together in Changsha or the kiss. *Our* kiss.

Our duties had pulled us further and further apart. At times, I would almost convince myself to stop dreaming, that there really wasn't anything more than those few long looks between us.

But then there were moments. Just small moments, but enough to make me wonder. It was infuriating and it was wonderful. I reached out now, trying to listen for the sound of him down below in the grass, but all I could hear were the sounds of the night buzzing all around.

13

"This lever reloads the chamber."

Satomi explained the parts of her rifle to Chang-wei while he hovered over her like a hummingbird over a flower.

But I wasn't jealous.

We were all seated in the wagon. The day had rolled along without incident. It was perfectly acceptable for the two of them to pass the time in conversation.

"It seems like the catch here would be prone to getting jammed."

"Chen-san, you underestimate my craftsmanship."

"I wouldn't dare, Sagara-san."

Yet. I wasn't jealous . . . yet. Even though their heads were bent close and they seemed to finish each other's sentences as if they were of one mind. Like Chang-wei, Satomi had an affinity for moving parts and joints and mechanisms, while I couldn't understand half of what they were saying.

"And the flintlock mechanism," Chang-wei went on. "It ignites very smoothly."

"My own design." Sagara Satomi was not a humble and timid

young lady. "My father originally adapted it from the Portuguese. I've tested it extensively. Less than one misfire per hundred."

"That one time could still get you killed," Chang-wei pointed out.

He spared a glance at me then. Something he saw made him pause, and he shot me a curious look. I quickly looked down at the book I'd been skimming.

Satomi was certainly pretty. She was also clever and skilled, and the two of them could speak of latches and springs and mechanisms until the stars came out. Turning the page, I studied an anatomical diagram of internal organs. I'd come back to this illustration again and again. Though I couldn't read the Japanese inscriptions, the book appeared to be detailing paths of electrical stimulation. There was another illustration of a parlor where a man appeared to be receiving treatment with an *elekiteru* device.

As I lifted the book to ask a question, an arrow embedded itself into the pages. I dropped the volume, startled.

"Get down!" Makoto shouted from the driver's seat.

I looked up as another arrow struck Yoshiro. Heart pounding, I ducked down in the wagon, crouching low and covering my head. It was a futile gesture. Arrows rained down upon us, one of them thudding into the board between Chang-wei and me.

Yoshiro jumped down from the driver's seat to shield Satomi with his body while I dragged myself over the side of the wagon, landing hard onto the dirt below. A heartbeat later, Chang-wei landed beside me. Together we huddled by the wheel, using the wagon as cover.

A chorus of snorts and grunts came from the mules, who started tugging at their harnesses. The wagon lurched about in jerking motions.

The shower of arrows ceased a moment later, but I remained frozen in place. Chang-wei looked at me. We were both breathing hard, and I could see the pulse throbbing in his neck. His eyes were sharp and alert. My heartbeat thudded against my rib cage, as if it would punch a hole through.

Makoto was on his feet, trying to calm the team as they paced and bucked in agitation. Arrows stood straight up in the surrounding field like a deadly harvest, and wooden shafts protruded from the wagon.

"Someone's coming," Makoto reported in a low growl. I heard the whisper of steel as he drew his sword.

Straightening, I could see figures approaching in the distance. Yoshiro drew his weapon and leapt onto the ground, squaring his shoulders for battle.

"Chen-san!" Satomi called.

She threw a rifle to Chang-wei and positioned herself to take aim with hers. I drew my pistol from my belt. I'd never fired a firearm before. It took both hands to cock it. Satomi had told me the weapon's range was short, but with the way things were headed, I had better be prepared.

"Your hand," Chang-wei remarked.

I frowned at him, not comprehending.

"It's not shaking." He moved to the rear of the wagon to take aim around the side.

My hands were indeed steady. The elegantly crafted pistol fit perfectly in my palm, and I was ready to use it if I had to. Though I was scared, my body seemed to remember. This wasn't the first time I'd been in an ambush. This wasn't the first time my life had been put in danger.

Hooking my arms onto the wagon, I pulled myself back up to it, using the spoke of the wheel as a foothold. Satomi was crouched at the opposite end, with her rifle steadied against the edge of the wagon. Yoshiro stood on the ground before her. An arrow protruded from his shoulder, but the pain didn't seem to bother him.

I'd seen men endure unimaginable injuries and still fight on when the fever of battle was upon them. The bodyguard appeared stone cold as his black eyes focused on the threat.

Staying low, I crawled over beside Satomi. "There are only three people approaching."

"There might be more in hiding," Satomi warned, staring down her barrel.

I put on the telescopic eyeglass and sighted in on the approaching men. "They appear unarmed," I reported.

Not a sword or rifle, as one might expect, or any other weapon in sight. One of them pointed out the wagon, and the three started waving their arms at us, shouting.

"One of them is turning around. He's running back out of the clearing."

"Getting reinforcements," Makoto said grimly.

The other two continued to advance, albeit cautiously.

"I think they wish to speak to us." I waved at them, returning their earlier signal. "Don't fire."

The lead man came forward, speaking rapidly. He sounded cross, or perhaps that was how all Japanese sounded to me.

"What is he saying?" I asked beneath my breath.

Makoto was already replying to the man while Satomi translated for Chang-wei and me. "He is declaring that this is the property of Lord Nabeshima of Saga domain. Didn't we see the notices about the testing?"

"Testing?" I asked as the man barked something at Makoto that I would characterize as haughty.

"For some new invention, I imagine. Takeda-sama is always working on one creation or another." Satomi relaxed and straightened, glancing around at the field of arrows surrounding us. "One can guess for what purpose."

THE INVENTOR'S villa was located on the outskirts of Saga

Clockwork Samurai 121

domain. We arrived that evening to the sight of three familiar-
looking men kneeling before the gate. I don't know how long they
had been there, but as soon as we arrived, the three fell to the
ground, prostrating themselves.

A middle-aged man appeared from the interior of the house.
He approached us, his dark robe brushing past the servants who
remained with their heads down.

"Takeda Hideyori offers his apologies to his honored guests."
Takeda , referred to himself by name as was custom "His
retainers were careless in executing their tasks."

He spoke using the Peking dialect, immediately marking our
origins. His words were crisply enunciated, with a distinctively
cultured tone. It was in contrast to the Canton hybrid dialect that
had evolved as a trading language.

Chang-wei similarly altered how he held himself, bowing at
the waist rigidly and introducing himself by name and rank. "It is
we who must apologize for arriving unannounced."

There was a prolonged exchange where Takeda repeated his
apology and Chang-wei responded by asking that the servants
not be punished. Takeda waved them away, and the men disappeared inside the villa, keeping their heads down as a show of
contrition.

The inventor turned his attention to Satomi. "Satomi-san."

"Takeda-sama."

They exchanged a few words in Japanese, but Takeda quickly
redirected the conversation back to us.

"Has any of your party suffered injury due to my careless-
ness?" he inquired.

I looked to Yoshiro, but Satomi's bodyguard seemed to have
recovered from his arrow wound, or rather he was bearing it
without complaint. I had offered to tend to him, but he refused.

"We are all well, Takeda-sama," Satomi replied.

"Allow me to offer a more appropriate welcome, then. You
must be tired."

Takeda invited us inside with a sweep of his arm, and Satomi stood back so Chang-wei could take the lead. The *karakuri* master and Chang-wei fell into conversation while the rest of us followed behind.

Lord Takeda was not remarkably tall, standing a little shorter than Chang-wei. Despite the opulent surroundings, his clothing was frugal in nature, dark robes that were clean and simple to the point of austere. His beard was neatly trimmed and threaded with gray, though his face was smooth with a decidedly pleasant expression.

He appeared to be a man who conducted himself with restraint. Someone who refrained from quick judgments and strong emotions. He and Chang-wei would get along well. They were still exchanging pleasantries ahead of us.

"I'm honored you have come from so far to see me," he was saying.

"Lady Sagara told us of your accomplishments."

"Satomi-san is too kind . . ."

Our host didn't question why we were sneaking around through open fields and ditches, nor remark on why we were outside of the trading settlement.

The interior wasn't divided into chambers like our courtyard houses. Instead the space was open, letting in the light through translucent paper windows on all sides. Various screens and sliding panels served as partitions, but a single glance allowed a winding view of the house.

"I sense good energy here," Chang-wei remarked as Takeda led us to a parlor area. "Balance."

I was thinking the same thing. There was a natural flow to the layout of the rooms. The space was sparsely decorated, and I could feel the tension of the road lifting from my shoulders as we walked through to the parlor.

The inventor seemed pleased with the remark. "It's very

peaceful here. Good for clearing the mind and letting new ideas in."

The sitting room had a view of the garden through wide door. Makoto and Yoshiro stayed back while Satomi, Chang-wei and I entered. We knelt on the floor upon bamboo mats around a low table.

The moment we were seated, a panel in the wall slid open and out came another one of the tea-serving *karakuri*. It glided onto the mat and came to a stop beside the table, bowing in charming fashion.

Takeda took the teapot from the tray, and the *karakuri* retreated.

"My guests usually expect such amusements from me," he admitted.

"There were *karakuri* servers in the teahouse we visited in the Chinese settlement," I told him.

"I fashioned those years ago. How good to hear they are still working."

I wondered if he knew of the teahouse's other activities. The clandestine meetings and secret passageways. The realization finally struck me—he'd probably built them.

"Takeda-sama is famous for creating these mechanical wonders," Satomi explained. "His works are in demand in every noble household."

"They're merely for amusement," the inventor insisted humbly. "Toys, more like. Fashions come and go among the Edo elite."

He held back the sleeve of his house robe to pour for each of us. Satomi then took the teapot to serve him in turn. I remembered what she had said about his proposal and how she'd fled. There was certainly an awkward familiarity about them now.

"There must be a spring mechanism in the mats," Chang-wei suggested before even touching his tea. "That's how the automatons are activated as soon as guests take a seat."

Takeda's eyes brightened. "A clever observation, Engineer Chen."

We drank our tea, which was a milder green variety, and spoke of inconsequential things. Chang-wei never spoke about the Ministry or any alliance, and Takeda didn't bring up the uncomfortable detail that we were foreigners roaming a land that had banned foreigners.

After tea, Takeda offered to show us more of his creations.

"We would be honored," Chang-wei replied, rising perhaps a little too quickly.

He was as eager as a child being offered sweets.

This time Satomi took the inventor's side as we left the parlor. We wound a path through the garden while they spoke quietly. I heard Yoshiro's name mentioned. The guardsman hovered nearby as always.

The stroll gave us a full view of the meticulous beauty of the garden; the trimmed bonsai trees and pebbled walkways. The babble of trickling water could be heard along with a rhythmic tapping that turned out to be some sort of a bamboo structure.

The fountain stood at one end of the garden and towered high above our heads. It was fashioned out of bamboo reeds interconnected with a series of levers and wheels. A spout poured water into a hollowed tube. When the weight of the water passed the tipping point, the tube would dip down, triggering a cascade of events—wheels turning, latches opening, levers shifting. The clack of bamboo could be heard at each contact point. A dance of motion that was both musical and hypnotic.

It was unnecessarily complex, yet completely enthralling.

"It's powered by hydraulics," Takeda explained. "Pressure drives water to the top of the tower, the falling motion of it driving all of the other actions."

He led us into a large bay at the rear of the villa and slid the door aside. The lanterns inside were already lit, and unlike the rest of the house, which appeared tidy and sparse, the workshop was an explosion of various machines and parts that would one day become machines.

It was a seductive state of clutter. So many places to look and explore. The mechanical creations were in various stages of completion. Books and scrolls lined an entire wall. Each corner and inch of the room begged for attention. Come see what is here!

I went to stand before a life-sized puppet of a dancer in a silk kimono, though it was probably incorrect to call her a puppet. There were no strings or sticks attached to her limbs.

The dancer's arms were raised and posed elegantly, as if waiting for the music to begin. Her face was painted with white makeup and her lips shaped in red tint. She was so lifelike that I imagined her eyes watching me even when I moved away.

A brass nightingale on a shelf ruffled metal wings and cooed at me when I walked by. Its jeweled eyes glinted as it cocked its head this way and that. The creature was so charming that I wanted to pick it up and turn it over and over with a child's curiosity. I didn't dare break anything.

One of the automatons was only partially complete. A panel had been removed from the left side of its chest, exposing the internal clockwork.

"I don't usually allow anyone to see the *karakuri* until they're completed," Takeda said, coming to stand beside me. "It ruins the illusion."

Reaching behind the *karakuri*, he released a trigger mechanism and the creation came to life. It lifted a bow and went through the motions of pulling an arrow from a quiver. The partial state of the automaton made it even more fascinating as I watched the exposed gears in the shoulder spinning to drive each movement.

"They're exquisite." I wanted to spend the rest of the day in this room, turning on each of the *karakuri* to find out their secrets.

"Was this the machine being tested in the field?" Chang-wei

asked from across the room. He stood over a workbench, looking down at a diagram sketched on a sheet of rice paper.

Takeda went to him, and I trailed immediately behind. This newest creation looked nothing like the collection inside the room. Over Chang-wei's shoulder, I could see a drawing of an assembly of bows rigged onto a base. A hook latched onto each string, and every hook was attached to an arm that could pull back the string in unison. It was a mechanical battery designed to fire a rain of arrows without needing a single archer.

"So this is the one design that interests you, Engineer Chen," Takeda observed. He sounded thoughtful and a little sad.

"I'm interested in all sorts of inventions."

"This one is meant to release a volley of arrows between rounds of gunfire. Rifles take a long time to reload, creating a vulnerable situation on the battlefield. This machine is for cover fire, not truly meant to be an accurate weapon. As you can see, the firing is quite blind."

All of his other machines were whimsical, meant to create an illusion to entice and amuse. But the arrow assembly was purely a war machine. There was no art to it.

"This one is very different from your other inventions, Takeda-san," I remarked with what I hoped was a respectful tone.

"The *karakuri* were part of my youth," he said, looking nostalgic. "In these times, it is important to be more practical in one's approach."

"Practical application is of utmost importance," Chang-wei agreed. "With foreign ships at our harbors, it's become a matter of life and death."

"Engineer Chen Chang-wei and Lady Jin Soling are from the imperial court of *Shina*," Satomi informed him.

"I deduced as much," Takeda said, letting out a breath. "What is it you seek, Chen-san?"

"An audience with the shogunate in Edo."

"Edo," Takeda echoed gravely. "Chen-san. Jin-san. I am very

happy you have come here. I have always been interested in learning from the discoveries of other lands. I've learned Dutch as well as Chinese for this very purpose. I've studied your developments with cannons and gunpowder engines with great interest. When Canton fell, I was horrified. How could the Middle Kingdom, the empire at the center of the world, be defeated by gaijin?"

"We were blind to our own failings," Chang-wei answered. "But now we can learn from those mistakes. We can learn together."

"Unfortunately, there is more than learning involved." Takeda turned to Satomi. "I apologize Satomi-san, if what I am about to say causes you more pain."

"I have had five years for any wounds to heal," Satomi replied, her jaw set in a hard line.

"After the Chinese Emperor capitulated, news came to us from the merchant ships. We learned of the devil ships powered by steam. We learned of how they rained fire and overpowered the coastal defenses. They won with barely an army released onto Chinese soil. This is an insulting assessment, is it not? I regret that there is no other way to say it."

"It's truth," Chang-wei said grimly. "It can't be helped."

"When the *bakufu* learned of what had happened, it merely reinforced what we had known for centuries. The foreigners had to be kept out at all costs. My good friend Lord Sagara protested when the *bakufu* decreed all foreigners found outside of the trading ports should be executed. Sagara-san paid for his conviction with his life."

Satomi's eyes remained dry, but she bowed her head.

"It wasn't the foreign warships the shogunate feared," Takeda continued. "By the time the ships came with their iron hulls and heavy cannons, it was already too late for the Chinese forces. The shogunate became convinced that we needed to protect against attempts to weaken us from within."

"The shogunate needed to protect the country against opium," I concluded.

"Against all foreign goods," Takeda conceded. "And foreign ideas. Our Chinese neighbors had become tainted in the eyes of the shogunate. So they tightened the restrictions on the trading ports, and any Western influence was seen as a threat. It became increasingly dangerous to be a scholar of foreign studies, so Lord Nabeshima invited me as a guest of his domain for my protection. He was a longtime admirer of my work."

"But he no longer wanted *karakuri*," Chang-wei finished for him. "He wanted war machines."

"The times require it. What good is knowledge if we don't use it? But as useful as my knowledge might be, I know I am merely a breath away from being declared a danger to the *bakufu*."

A sinking feeling formed in the pit of my stomach. "We've endangered you by coming here."

Takeda shook his head. "No. This is what makes me dangerous." He gestured to the books on the shelves. "And this."

He pointed to the clockwork devices and the tools hung over the workbench.

"These are ideas from the outside, from the West, but I can't unlearn what is in my head. I can't undo what my hands have done. I don't wish to. That, in itself, would be death."

14

Outside of the workshop, talk turned to less dire topics. Takeda did not mention traveling to Edo on our behalf, but he didn't banish us from his villa, either.

After our brief tour of the grounds, we were shown to our rooms. The villa was staffed by relatively few servants. I wondered if Takeda's *karakuri* had other functions within the household, reducing the need for attendants.

Satomi and I were lodged together in a sleeping room on the main courtyard while Chang-wei and Makoto were given a room on the other side of the house. Before our evening meal, Satomi led to me to the bathhouse where we scrubbed clean before sinking into a steam bath.

I closed my eyes and let the heat soak into my muscles. The coals burning beneath the platform kept the water just below scalding. At first the heat of it was a shock, but gradually I could feel the tension and cares of the outside world melting away. The house really did have a meditative quality about it, from the gardens to the delicate walls and paper windows, which allowed light to filter through.

"Takeda-sama will come around to your cause."

I opened my eyes to see Satomi regarding me through the steam. Her bare shoulders rose above the water.

"He'll take us to Edo to address the shogunate?" I asked.

"Perhaps Edo is not yet ready for that."

"Peking isn't ready, either." Emperor Yizhu had refused to open formal talks with Japanese.

"But with time, things can change. Takeda-sama will be a good ally for you. He's well respected." She rested her head back against the edge of the pool and closed her eyes. "My father wanted cooperation between our two countries. Unfortunately, he wasn't as diplomatic as Takeda Hideyori."

"Lord Takeda is a good man," I agreed. "Well-mannered, educated and clever as well."

Satomi angled a slanted look at me, her eyes still half lidded. "Are you going to suggest that I would have been wise to marry him after all?"

"I wasn't thinking that."

She visibly relaxed, sinking back into the bath. "It's not that I mind being around people. But wherever I go, the sentiment is the same. I should be grateful for Takeda-sama's protection. That he was offering me a secure future. No future is secure."

"Lord Takeda doesn't say such things."

"He doesn't. Takeda-sama has been nothing but kind," she agreed. "He also prefers men."

The last part was added as an afterthought.

"Oh," I replied. "Oh."

Satomi was the one living within an isolated country, yet I was the one who felt sheltered and unworldly.

"Anyone who doesn't believe the Westerners will eventually come to our shores is blind. Even the most reactionary members of the *bakufu* know that," Satomi continued. "But we've enjoyed peace for so long that we believe we can prevail on our own."

"What do *you* believe?"

She paused as she considered it. "I've been alone for a long time now. Maybe it's time to look outside of myself."

It wasn't an answer, but in a way it was. She had come with us here, hadn't she?

"There is a phrase in our language for a kind of fate that causes people to meet. We call it *yuan fen*," I told her.

Satomi nodded. "We call it *en*."

"I believe the work of our fathers and their deaths created fate between us. You and I were meant to meet, Satomi. We were meant to do something besides grieve for those we've lost."

I caught her brushing the back of her hand hastily over her eyes. "Whoever heard of a daughter continuing her father's legacy?" she said bitingly.

Though we had just met, I felt close to her. It made me suddenly bold. "I also believe there is more to my father's execution than I've been told."

"Why is that?"

I told her about the Japanese puzzle box that had been hidden from my father's possessions and the device contained within it.

"They were sending messages using the signal towers," I surmised. "Sharing knowledge."

Satomi pressed a hand to her temples, thinking hard. "They might have tried to form an alliance back then."

"Do you have any of your father's records?"

"At the school. After the assassination, they seized his lands, but the school was left alone. No one cared."

"Maybe we can finally find out what it was they communicated across the ocean," I proposed. "We can finish what they started."

∾

ON THE WAY TO SUPPER, I ran into Chang-wei in the garden. At first I didn't recognize him. He was wearing a plain robe, a loose *yukata* that fell to his ankles. The garment was dyed in a blue workman's color. His hair was damp from the bathhouse.

It was strange to see him in Japanese clothing. The garment appeared archaic, like a traditional Han robe of centuries past. I had been given a house robe as well so that I was no longer dressed like a boy.

"Soling," he began.

"Chang-wei. What's the matter?" His gaze had that faraway look that meant he was pondering something.

"Nothing." Chang-wei's jaw was clenched too tight as he smoothed his sleeve over his arm.

"Lady Sagara went to see to her bodyguard," I told him as we walked together through the garden. "He's resting to recover from his wound."

"The rest will do him good. He rarely sleeps, that one."

"He's very dedicated to Lady Sagara's protection."

Yoshiro was exactly how I imagined a samurai would be. Taciturn. Uncompromising. Honor until death.

"A loyal friend," Chang-wei agreed.

I suspected it was more than that. A man and a woman running away together immediately spoke of forbidden love, even if Satomi was of a different class than the swordsman. I kept quiet on the matter—it was rude to spread gossip.

"Soling, you . . . you're a good friend," he began haltingly.

"Of course."

"If I were to ask— If something were to happen . . ."

I hung on every word, but Chang-wei couldn't get his thoughts together. "Never mind."

He was so *impossible*. "Whatever it is—"

"Forget I said anything. It was nothing important."

He was lying. Or not telling the truth. Was I supposed to beg it out of him?

"They're waiting for us." He gestured toward the far side of the garden.

Impossible.

The sliding panel of the main parlor room remained open to the garden, and two lanterns had been lit on either side of the entrance. Makoto and Lord Takeda were engaged in conversation, but Takeda stood to greet us as we set foot on the walkway. Satomi was the last to arrive to supper, without her bodyguard. She almost seemed incomplete without his dark shadow beside her.

"Makoto-san and I were discussing the Great Sword Hunt," Takeda told us after directing his servants to bring the evening meal. "When the shogunate decreed that all commoners must relinquish their swords. They also sought to chase out *rōnin* from villages and towns."

Makoto stiffened at the mention of *rōnin*. I hadn't realized the word held such power, but of course it did. It was a word that indicated a different class of men. Ones who had been stripped of honor and cast out.

"The sword hunts further romanticized the idea of the blade as the symbol of nobility and status," Takeda told us.

"The sword is not merely a symbol," Makoto argued. "A thousand swords can conquer a city."

"And a thousand firearms can topple a regime," Satomi countered. She gave Chang-wei a knowing look that I wasn't particularly fond of. "That is why the shogunate fears them so."

Makoto's shoulders straightened as he rested a hand onto the hilt of his weapon. "There is honor in wielding a sword. The decision of life or death resides with the swordsman. There is little art or skill in the making of a gun or the pulling of a trigger."

Satomi raised an eyebrow. "Efficiency is art. Achieving one's purpose is skill."

"Thank you both for educating us in your ways," I interjected, "with this peaceful discussion of opposing views."

They both looked at me, suddenly remembering there were guests in their midst. Makoto sank back a notch, and Satomi lifted her wine to take a sip. I prayed there would be no sudden duel between them.

Takeda used the break to address Chang-wei and me. "In the early days of the Tokugawa, every army was equipped with firearms. A battle could not be won without a battery of them. But for the last two hundred years, those weapons have been confiscated and left to rust. When the Chinese ports fell, a few among the samurai class counseled the *bakufu* to arm itself with firearms. We were scientists as well as samurai and had studied Western technology and warfare. Because of that, our views were unpopular."

"The samurai have elevated themselves to godly status," Satomi said with a curl in her lip. "But they've had no one to fight but themselves for two centuries."

Makoto's expression was like stone. "The katana is indeed a weapon for a civilized age."

He claimed to no longer be samurai, but honor and pride still ran thick in his blood.

Takeda folded his hands before him. "If there is poison in the water and one knows of it, it is his responsibility to inform the villagers. If the villagers will not believe him, it is his responsibility to destroy the well. Even if he is condemned for it. Silence is not loyalty. I will petition the *bakufu* on your behalf, Engineer Chen. I truly believe you have both of our kingdoms' best interests in mind."

Chang-wei bowed low. "*Arigato gozaimasu*, Takeda-sama. If you'll allow me, I'd like to accompany you so the shogunate will know the strength of our intentions."

I bit back a protest. Edo was already unfavorable to foreigners. Once in the capital, we would be surrounded on all sides with escape routes cut off. Moreover, the imperial court had refused to support an official diplomatic mission. Even if the

Emperor could intervene on our behalf, he would consider us a lost cause and be done with us.

The inventor folded his hands and breathed deeply as he considered Chang-wei's request.

"Therein lies the challenge," he began with a rueful smile. "You see, I have not set foot outside this villa for five years now. The moment I leave without permission, there will be a bounty on my head."

Satomi looked startled. "Takeda-sama—"

"It was good of you to leave when you did, Satomi-san. And there was a good reason I did not come to find you, even though I was your guardian. I am under house arrest."

Chang-wei stiffened, glancing out to the garden. "Are we being watched?"

Takeda nodded calmly. "The servants will have sent word to Lord Nabeshima of my visitors. There is no need to fear. The daimyo assures me that this confinement is for my own protection. I believe it is to keep me away from the corrupting foreign influences in Nagasaki, lest my reputation be further darkened. Once Lord Nabeshima learns of your presence, I will be expected to explain myself, which I will. So there is no need to make the long journey to Edo. The *bakufu* will come to us."

"Then we will make our case to Lord Nabeshima," Chang-wei said, though I could see the tension gathering in his shoulders. The tranquil villa had become a trap. "Our purpose was to make contact with the shogunate. We have nothing to hide."

"And that it why I trust you, Engineer Chen. A samurai's sense of honor, wouldn't you say, Makoto-san?"

Makoto's reply was to drink his rice wine in silence.

"Let us eat, then," Takeda invited as the servants returned with plates of rice and fish. "We have an important day ahead of us."

15

I awoke in the middle of the night not knowing what time it was. Moonlight filtered into the sleeping chamber through the open windows. Beside me, Satomi slept soundly.

As I lay on the padded futon, a sound came from just outside my window. Someone was outside, walking with a slow, deliberate gait. Clutching my blanket, I lay perfectly still, listening.

There was definitely someone out there in the garden. Crawling over to Satomi, I took hold of her shoulder, clamping a hand over her mouth as she gasped.

"Listen," I whispered.

Satomi raised herself onto one arm. The footsteps came closer, and a great hulking shadow passed by the edge of the windowed panel. We couldn't make out anything through the rice paper. At first I thought it might have been Yoshiro, patrolling the garden in his armor, but there was an odd quality to the footsteps. They were heavy, with a clang of metal at each step. Then we saw a glint of armor as the figure passed by the window.

"*Hitokiri!*" Satomi hissed, reaching beneath her mattress. Her hand emerged gripping a pistol. "Get up."

Another set of footsteps could be heard, each one like a

metal weight dropping. I threw on my robe and tied the sash hastily, while my heart pounded out of my chest. My hands trembled as I fumbled for the gun Satomi had given me. Whatever was out there seemed more demon than human. Makoto had described these killers as if they were otherworldly. Now I knew why.

Satomi slung her rifle over her shoulder and shoved her feet into her boots. "Once we get out, you run. Don't stand and fight, just run."

Her advice might have been the wisest course, but it didn't matter. I had to find Chang-wei.

"Listen." Satomi grabbed my arm as we headed toward the sliding door. "I meant what I said. They won't come after you if you aren't the one they were sent to kill."

I forced myself to take a breath. "What if we all are marked for death?" I whispered back at her.

"Run," Satomi insisted, with a finality that left my blood cold.

I slid the panel open and took a moment to assess the courtyard. It appeared empty, so Satomi and I slipped outside. Now we were faced with a dilemma—shout and alert the others? Or stay silent in hopes of sneaking by the assassins?

As quickly as I could, I ran over the grass and slipped behind the bamboo sculpture. Satomi followed immediately behind me, crouching low to hide. Then I saw one of them.

He was wearing a suit of armor fashioned from interlocking steel plates. The suit encased him, increasing his height and breadth to inhuman proportions. It was hard to believe anything with a heart and soul resided inside that cage.

Satomi turned toward the main part of the residence. "I have to get to Takeda-sama."

"What happened to running?"

"I owe him my life."

I followed her as she slipped into the house. We wound through unlit passages, our feet whispering over the tatami mats.

Satomi was familiar with the layout, having lived there, but I was following blind.

We emerged in another part of the garden only to see one of the metal warriors sliding the panel door open to a sleeping chamber.

Without a word, Satomi unslung the rifle from her shoulder. "You go on. This is not your fight."

"Wait."

I pointed to the other end of the garden where a faint light shone through the trees. Lord Takeda's workshop.

Forgetting stealth, we ran through the garden toward the workshop while the assassin was occupied within the chamber. Lanterns glowed from inside, bright as day. Satomi pulled the door open, and we both entered, closing the door behind us even though it provided little cover.

Takeda wasn't working on any of his creations. Instead, he sat cross-legged on the floor before a low table with a scroll laid out before him. He had a calligraphy brush in hand, and a stream of characters flowed from the tip of it onto the paper. He paused to look up at us, then addressed Satomi in Japanese.

Whatever she said back to him rang with defiance.

The inventor turned to me next. "You must tell her to go. Both of you. There isn't much time."

Satomi refused to back down. "You come with us, Takeda-sama. Or both our deaths will be on your head."

I bit back my reply. I wasn't yet ready to die tonight, for honor or any other sacrifice, but Satomi's ruse had worked. With a deep sigh, Takeda rolled up his scroll and rose. "Then we must hurry."

He ushered us toward a storage room in the back. It was good that we'd come for him. It provided a way for him to go yet still maintain honor.

"That scroll case, there." He gestured toward the highest shelf. "We need to take that with us."

Without asking any questions, I moved to retrieve the case. It proved to be too high, and Satomi pushed one of the crates over to use as a stepladder.

"The *hitokiri* will be coming this way," she urged. "What's so import—"

The door swung shut behind us, and the lock clicked on the other side. Cursing, Satomi rushed to the door and pounded her fist against it.

"Takeda-sama!"

He hushed her from the other side. "Quiet. I'll draw them away."

Then he spoke to her a final phrase in Japanese. At that, the sliver of light filtering in from beneath the door dimmed before going completely dark. We heard the sound of footsteps retreating.

Satomi spat out a curse. I heard the click of gun being cocked. A moment later, there was a flash of light followed by an explosion that shook the door. One more shot and the lock was destroyed.

She shoved the door aside and stepped out. Over her shoulder, I saw the armored assassin entering the darkened workshop. A flicker of metal sliced through the air, rattling like an iron snake. I didn't know what was happening, but instinct kicked in. I jumped left while Satomi threw herself to the right.

Our instincts proved correct. A blade thudded into the door behind us, only to be yanked back a moment later.

It was a curved blade attached to a chain. I ducked behind the *karakuri* dancer only to have the blade embed itself into the automaton's chest. Right where the heart would be. The *karakuri* clattered to the floor as the blade was jerked backward.

Blood pulsed hot through my veins as I scrambled toward the next automaton. This one had the silhouette of a warrior, but it was far outshadowed by the demon that stalked toward me. Metal boots clanged over the floorboards. The assassin held a chained weapon in his hands, and his armor formed an outer skeleton that made him impervious to attack.

It was hard to believe there was a man inside that monstrosity. The protective suit that encased him was reminiscent of dragon scales, and his face was covered with an ornate helmet and mask. I had imagined assassins would come in the night, slipping in and out like smoke, but there was nothing quiet or hidden about these killers. *Hitokiri* met their victims face-to-face and struck fear in their hearts.

I slipped a hollow bamboo reed from my sash and broke the paper seal on each end. The blow tube was a weapon I had developed during those long hours with the medicine cabinets in the Court of Physicians, but it required patience. The target had to be close.

My palms began to sweat as the assassin neared. The thought of taking my last breath here, among these broken creations, left my blood cold. These killers knew nothing about who I was, nor did they care. If I was stricken down, I would die among strangers in a foreign land. The thought left me hollowed.

When I heard the metal footsteps on the other side of the *karakuri*, I stood and aimed the bamboo tube. I blew hard into the end of it, and a cloud of fine dust erupted between us and enveloped the assassin. The blinding powder had the additional benefit of being able to slip through the mask, burning against skin and eyes. The *hitokiri* grabbed at his face, grunting and coughing—the first signs that my adversary was indeed human.

I drew my pistol, but before I could fire, the air crackled around me. Blue white lightning danced over the steel plate armor of the assassin, illuminating him in silhouette. Then all went dark, and he crashed to the floor. Satomi stood behind the fallen warrior, wearing what looked like a spiked glove on one hand. Our eyes met.

Without a word, we were running again, shoving past the *karakuri* automatons to emerge into the night air.

"Is he dead?" I asked, referring to the assassin.

"Perhaps," Satomi replied coldly. "This weapon is particularly suited against that armor they hide themselves in."

Moonlight revealed the copper wire that twisted over her glove. She removed it and shoved it away in her pack.

There were two *hitokiri* from what I had seen, and maybe more. With one behind us, there was still at least one stalking the villa. By now, my eyes were adjusted to the darkness, and I spotted Takeda standing among the boulders in the sand garden. He made no effort to hide or run as another warrior encased in heavy armor emerged from the villa.

The *hitokiri* swiveled his iron helmet in Takeda's direction and stalked forward, intent on his victim. The clang of armored footsteps formed an ominous cadence.

Satomi raised her rifle. "I'm too far away," she muttered even as she took aim.

A shot rang out, shattering the night, and the armored *hitokiri* staggered backward. Satomi lowered her rifle, startled. Her weapon had never fired.

Chang-wei stood with his rifle aimed at the other end of the garden. The first shot was followed by another one, which sent the assassin crashing back through the wood and paper paneling of the main parlor.

We broke into a run. By the time we reached Takeda, Chang-wei had taken hold of him by the front of his robe. Makoto stood ready beside them with his sword drawn.

"Where is everyone else?" The rooms all around us remained dark and silent. None of the servants had come out to investigate the commotion.

"The servants were all ordered away," Takeda replied, his expression grim. He alone remained calm among us. Too calm. Had he known about the attack? Or had he simply anticipated it?

"We need to go."

Chang-wei's sharp command brought us all back to attention.

There was movement among the rubble of the wall as the assassin stirred. The joints of his body suit creaked as he rolled onto his knees. His armor had managed to stop both shots.

Makoto took the lead with Satomi and Lord Takeda immediately behind him. Chang-wei took my side, a look of concern on his face. I nodded at him to let him know I was unharmed. There was no time for any more than that. The hired killer was back on his feet, and the suit of armor slowed him down, but only fraction of what it should have.

As we made our way toward the gate, another armored figure blocked our path, but it was Yoshiro this time. The bodyguard drew his sword and moved past us, making a direct line toward the *hitokiri*.

Satomi glanced at him only once.

"Run," she commanded as the first clash of steel rang through the courtyard behind us.

We fled without looking back.

THE SURROUNDING FIELDS provided little cover, so we continued on foot through the night, trudging on for hours before finally taking shelter by a hillside. There we huddled without a fire.

"I'll take first watch," Makoto said. "Get some rest."

I doubted any of us would be able to sleep. I would have nightmares about steel-clad *hitokiri* appearing to cut me into ribbons.

We hadn't had time to take any warmer clothing, and I shivered as the chill set in through the light house robe. Chang-wei's arm closed around me.

"You can lean against me," he said in my ear.

There was nothing suggestive about it. His other hand remained on his rifle, which he'd reloaded as soon as he had the chance.

I laid my head against his chest and closed my arms around him, grateful for his warmth and the steady beat of his heart beneath my ear. Though I had thought I was too anxious to sleep, I drifted off holding on to Chang-wei. The battle and escape from the villa had drawn every last bit of energy from me.

When I woke up, it was morning. My head rested in Chang-wei's lap with him nodded asleep over me. His eyes were closed, and his hand rested lightly in my hair. His breathing was slow and heavy.

An argument was already in full force nearby. It was in Japanese, which had a tendency to sound a bit angry to me in general. Satomi and Lord Takeda were discussing something, and his steady tone intermingled with her more heated arguments. Makoto interjected with an occasional remark. The three of them were likely discussing our next move while Chang-wei and I were left out.

Chang-wei stirred above me. A frown crossed his face before he opened his eyes, as if the coming day were a puzzle to be solved and he was already preparing himself.

"You're awake," he said, his voice heavy with sleep.

His hand remained in my hair as he straightened, wincing at the stiffness in his neck. He glanced about to take account of our surroundings and of the discussion broiling nearby before looking back down at me.

"You're all right?" he asked.

It was more than a polite inquiry. His eyes searched mine, and I could see the concern in his face. "I'm fine."

He finally removed his hand from my hair, and it was a good time to get up, though I wouldn't have minded staying in his lap awhile longer. But we were fugitives and needed to move quickly.

Chang-wei turned to address the others. "Excuse my interruption, but it is my opinion that it would be very dangerous to travel to Saga Castle under the current circumstances."

"See, the *Shina-jin* agrees with me," Satomi said. "Takeda-sama no longer has Lord Nabeshima's protection, otherwise the *hitokiri* wouldn't have attacked us in his domain."

"If that is true, then all the more reason for me to go explain myself to the daimyo," the inventor insisted.

"Takeda-sama would be walking to his death, same as my father." Satomi rose to her feet. "I apologize for my impertinence, but I won't allow that."

Anger filled every step as she walked to the edge of our camp to look out over the fields beyond. Something about her standing there all alone struck a chord deep within me. Satomi seemed so desolate, holding on to her firearm as if she could single-handedly fend off the world with it.

Then I realized why she looked so vulnerable. Yoshiro, her faithful servant, had stayed behind to allow our escape. Rarely had I seen her without him by her side, silent, but ever present. I couldn't bear to think of Yoshiro as gone, though I'd barely known him.

"We have an airship docked in Nagasaki," Chang-wei began. "If we can return to the Chinese quarter safely, I can offer you passage aboard it."

"And how do you plan to smuggle a prominent scientist aboard your ship?" Makoto asked. "By then, the trade authority will be alerted to Takeda-sama's escape."

Chang-wei fought to maintain his composure, though I could see his jaw tense. "The settlement will provide us some cover. We'll be among Chinese merchants."

"You underestimate the shogunate's influence in the settlement."

Takeda laid a book across his knees as he considered the options. It must have been the same one he was writing in as he prepared to meet his ancestors. Just like the night before, he showed no fear, merely a calm sense of resignation.

"No one who leaves our land is allowed to return," he

declared. "If he attempts to do so, he is immediately put to death."

Japanese law was harsh, but that was their way. No exceptions. No compromises. What was more intriguing was their ability to enforce their laws. From what I little I knew of the three Japanese before me, the laws were enforced not only by the authorities, but by the very will of the people.

"There will be a place for Takeda-sama in the Ministry of Science," Chang-wei promised. "A man with your learning will always have a place."

"As an informant. A traitor," Takeda declared. "Someone who knows what I know—the *bakufu* will not relinquish their hold easily. They may not want my knowledge, but they don't want anyone else to have it."

"Then live in the provinces as a scholar and scientist," I said. "We won't force you to join the imperial court."

Chang-wei shot me a warning look, but I ignored it. We weren't here to press anyone into service.

"The *hitokiri* are no common mercenaries," Makoto pointed out. "They are special assassins, commanded by the *bakufu*. If they have come for you, then you have been labeled an enemy of the shogunate."

"What Makoto-san means to say is that I am already named as a traitor," Takeda said. "I can either die a good death as a samurai or willingly become *rōnin*. There is no other option."

"We'll go together." Satomi remained apart from us. Her voice seemed to come from far away, as if her spirit remained distant as well. "Perhaps it was always fate that this would happen."

Something flickered behind Takeda's tranquil expression as he regarded her. I don't know how he faced life and death with such calm. Perhaps it came with age, or with a warrior's training.

Slowly, he rose to his feet. "It is decided, then. I have no master."

"No master but yourself," Satomi corrected, finally coming back to join us.

"You would be surprised what one can accomplish as a man cast adrift," Makoto said, refraining from his usual cynical smirk. "But first there's the business of making it back to Nagasaki alive."

16

Wtraveled south, traipsing through muddy fields and constantly on watch. Without our wagon, we had lost all of our supplies. By midday we were all starving.

Makoto managed to dig up a few wild yams. An attempt to spear fish from a stream set us back an hour with no fish to speak of. We ended up setting up a makeshift lure made of silk cut from our clothing. The trap had little chance of working, but it gave us some hope while we waited for our humble meal of wild yams to cook over the fire.

The area was shaded and partially hidden by the growth of trees and brush that naturally thrived near a water source. The water was cool and rejuvenating, at least. I splashed it over my face while I completed a simple calculation in my head.

"It's been five days since we've been gone from the Chinese quarter. Do you think anyone will have taken notice?"

Chang-wei didn't seem too concerned. "We are two of a thousand," he assured. "And Captain Zhao will cover for us."

He acted as if he had no fear of being caught. As if he wanted to be arrested and dragged before the shogun to plead his cause. It was more likely he'd be thrown into a dank cell in the local prison with rats for company.

"It was bold of you to promise passage to Peking," I pointed out.

"Lord Takeda is a brilliant scientist. He would be a great asset to our cause."

"At the price of forsaking his country and his honor."

"I'm not unsympathetic to his plight." Chang-wei's voice rose a notch, one of the few times he'd raised it. He immediately brought it back under control. "But we have to think of greater things. The survival our both of our nations. Takeda knows this."

Lord Takeda sat on a flat boulder, reading through his scroll. Satomi sat with her back to him, cleaning and oiling her rifle. The two of them made an odd pair indeed. Once we reached Nagasaki safely, we would have to smuggle them aboard the airship.

Would the imperial court regard them any better than the shogunate regarded us? The Ministry would value their knowledge, for certain; Satomi with her firearms and Takeda's ingenuity and scientific knowledge. I hated to think how they would be exploited by the Emperor.

"What if you and I were stranded in Nagasaki?" I asked.

"It won't happen," Chang-wei replied.

"I'm not saying it *will* happen. I'm just saying what if it did?"

"It's pointless to imagine far-fetched scenarios," he said irritably.

"It may not be so far-fetched if you consider it," I countered, feeling a bit of irritation myself.

Not until I asked did I realize this was a very realistic scenario, perhaps more realistic than us smuggling a prominent scientist and inventor as well as a gunsmith to Peking.

I failed to string Chang-wei into continuing the conversation.

When the yams were cooked, he tried to offer me his half, claiming he wasn't hungry. I don't know if it was meant at a peace offering, but it only made me more irritable.

"You don't have to be self-sacrificing for my sake," I told him.

"It's the truth. I'm not feeling hungry," he insisted.

Heat rose up the back of my neck. I was hungry and tired and very irritable, but at least I was honest about it. I was about to snap at him, but then I noticed he did appear a little pale. Even though it was cool in the shade, I noticed him wipe sweat off his brow. Had he fallen ill?

"You should eat to keep up your strength," I nagged gently. "I don't want to have to carry you."

He granted me a small smile at that. "Soling—"

"Yes?"

I waited for what he meant to say, listening so intently that I heard a faint rattle of metal over the bubbling of the stream. I turned to Takeda and saw a dark silhouette emerging from the woods.

"Get down!"

The scream had just left my lips when the chain snaked through the air. Satomi grabbed the inventor by the robe and tugged sharply. They both toppled off of the boulder just as the blade struck, sparks flying against the rock with the force of the blow.

Chang-wei and I sprung to our feet as another assassin emerged behind us. One more entered the fray to advance upon Makoto. Makoto drew his sword and prepared for attack.

Three against five, but the *hitokiri* were trained killers. They had discarded their steel suits in favor of stealth. The armor would have slowed them down and alerted us of their presence. Instead each was dressed in a simple black kimono with chest and arm guards.

The image of their faces was more frightening than seeing

their masks. They showed no more emotion than their facial armor had shown. Each expression was as cold and hard as stone. Each rigid stare showed the depth of their conviction. They would be victorious today or die trying.

Chang-wei dragged me behind him and leveled his rifle at the *hitokiri* closest to us. There would be no negotiation. Without hesitation, Chang-wei pulled the trigger. The impact of the shot jammed the rifle against his shoulder, and he fell back a step.

The assassin reeled backward, struck in the center of his chest. He regained his feet with a deathly glare, his look disdainful. One bullet was far from enough to kill a *hitokiri*.

The ring of steel on the other side of the stream told me Makoto had engaged. Amidst the chaos, Takeda shouted something at the attackers.

A command? An attempt at negotiation?

Takeda stood unarmed as the *hitokiri* approached with sword drawn. It was like a ritual, unfolding with a sense of pattern and inevitability. Satomi scrambled to reach her rifle, which had fallen into the water.

"When you find an opening, run, Soling," Chang-wei insisted. He raised his rifle in both hands to wield it like a staff as he faced off against our attacker.

Instead of wasting my energy arguing with Chang-wei, I drew my pistol from my sash. One shot at close range. I would make it count.

Behind us, Satomi reached her firearm and took aim just as the *hitokiri* raised his sword to strike Takeda down. The flintlock struck with a harmless click.

The firing mechanism must have flooded in the water.

"Satomi!"

She looked over in time to catch my pistol. Swinging around, she positioned her arm and fired.

The crack of the shot caused everyone to freeze. Takeda's

attacker stood still, sword held high. The look on his face had gone blank, and it took me two heartbeats before I saw the wound in the center of his forehead. It was nothing more than a dot, too neat and clean to be a death blow.

But it was.

The *hitokiri* fell to his knees before collapsing. A pile of flesh and bone with spirit gone, but there was no time to mourn or celebrate. Takeda stood over the body and calmly retrieved the assassin's sword. Once it was in his hands, Takeda transformed from scholar to warrior.

Chang-wei's attacker charged, and he parried the strike against the barrel of his rifle. The sword flashed back without pause, slicing across Chang-wei's arm. He fell back with a hiss of pain as blood flowed from the cut.

The assassin advanced forward, death caged in steel, sword raised high. Chang-wei's name caught in my throat. This couldn't be happening. This couldn't be the end.

The blade never fell. The *hitokiri* paused as his cold gaze scanned over Chang-wei.

It was all Chang-wei needed. He'd managed to hold on to the rifle and swung the barrel forward now, firing blindly.

A black plume of smoke momentarily blocked our attacker from view, but the swordsman emerged through the cloud unscathed. Satomi and Takeda regrouped beside me while Chang-wei fell back with his hand clutched to his wound. For the first time, I looked into the assassin's eyes and saw death. My death. The death of my friends.

There were only two things to do, fight or run. I was no warrior, so I prepared to run when a hulking figure came crashing through the brush.

"*Yoshiro,*" Satomi gasped as her loyal bodyguard charged toward us.

His armor had torn away in places, and there was a knife

stuck in his chest, but he still held his sword. The assassin turned just in time to see the warrior bearing down on him. Yoshiro clubbed the other man against the side of side head. The move was more blunt force than skill, but it sent the assassin to the ground.

The other *hitokiri* broke away to join his comrade. Behind him I saw Makoto kneeling on the ground with his hand clutched to his midsection. He was wounded. How badly, I couldn't tell.

The remaining assassin crossed swords with Yoshiro while his comrade crawled onto his hands and knees. Blood flowed from the man's temple, but he was far from finished.

"We must go now," Takeda said.

He pulled Satomi away as the assassins regrouped. I ran to Makoto, ignoring Chang-wei's shouting behind me. When I came to him, the hand pressed to his ribs was drenched in blood. The other one still gripped the katana.

"Go," Makoto said through gritted teeth. "My fight isn't over yet."

Over my shoulder, Yoshiro was holding the assassins off. My stomach sickened as a blade sliced across his ribs, but the body-guard didn't flinch as he renewed his attack. Makoto struggled to his feet with a hiss of pain. If he returned to battle, it would only be to die a warrior's death.

"Come," Chang-wei said grimly. "There's no time."

He took Makoto's sword arm to drag him toward the rest of our party. With a curse, Makoto shoved Chang-wei aside and sheathed his sword. Of the two of them, Makoto was more heavily injured. At least they were both able to move on their own power.

We went as quickly as we could. Makoto pushed on through gritted teeth as we climbed the next rise. Chang-wei looked pale as well.

We reached the next rise before Satomi dared to look back. From the distance, the warriors appeared like tiny dolls by the stream. I had prayed silently during our escape that Yoshiro would manage to prevail and find us once more, but one glimpse at the stream told me it had been wishful thinking.

Yoshiro had fallen to his knees by the water. He offered no resistance as the *hitokiri* raised his sword and cut clean through his neck. For a moment we all stared, unable to comprehend what had happened as his head rolled on the ground. His body fell a beat afterward in an absurd and awful moment.

"We need to go," Satomi said finally, her voice choked. "It's done."

No more than a few seconds had passed, but it felt like a lifetime. Satomi's eyes glistened as she turned to search for a way down the hilltop. Takeda reached out to touch a hand to her shoulder, and they exchanged a look between them. She nodded quietly back at him, and the five of us continued on with Chang-wei and me supporting Makoto between us.

BY THE TIME we reached the rice fields outside of Nagasaki domain, every last drop of will within us had dried up. The terraced hillsides stretched out unending to the horizon in every direction, which allowed us to scan for attack. We were safe for the moment, but it wouldn't last.

Lord Takeda ushered us into a storehouse standing among the paddies. The structure was built of wood and raised onto stilts to avoid the damp earth. We climbed up and found the interior empty, but thankfully warm and dry.

Chang-wei and I laid Makoto out on the floor while Takeda folded a paper lantern and sparked the wick inside, holding it over us. I bent to see to Makoto's wound. We hadn't been able to do more than keep pressure against it while we fled.

"It's not bad," Makoto insisted as I pulled back the folds of his robe.

Despite his words, his knuckles were clenched white by his sides. The assassin's blade had sliced cleanly through three layers of cloth as well as a layer of muscle. The gash in his abdomen welled up with blood, and I could sense the bile rising in my throat. I fought back a wave of dizziness.

He's not bleeding out, I told myself. It couldn't be deep. I hoped it wasn't deep.

"I don't have much experience treating wounds," I confessed.

For some reason, my mind strayed to my usual task of mixing fertility potions, and I pressed the back of my hand against my mouth to keep from laughing. To keep from crying. I could do this.

Using a knife, I tore out strips of cloth from the hem of my robe and used them to stanch the blood and inspect the wound carefully. I didn't know about cuts and stabs, but I knew the body. I knew the major arteries and veins and signs of damage.

"None of his organs have been pierced," I said shakily. "But the cut has torn across muscle. We have to keep it clean and stop the bleeding."

"Should we stitch the cut?" Satomi asked.

I shook my head. "It will need to drain. I'll bind it tight to help the wound seal itself."

I set to work wrapping his entire midsection with a broad swath of cloth. I needed to stabilize the surrounding area so the wound wouldn't reopen when he moved.

"He needs to rest. Remain still while the cut heals." Even as I said it, I knew it wasn't possible.

"We have a few hours at most," Takeda warned.

Makoto had suffered other injuries as well. A stab wound to his leg that he'd surprisingly not complained about, and numerous cuts over his arms. One strike had come perilously close to his neck but instead glanced over his shoulder, slicing through skin, but nothing vital. His black kimono hid the damage, but I could see the story of the fight now, with the *hitokiri* cutting him down bit by bit.

"That's what *hitokiri* means," Makoto said as I tried to stop the bleeding. "Man cutter. I was lucky to survive the first blow."

I tried to keep my face blank as I tended to him. "You should conserve your energy."

"Talking distracts me." His complexion had gone pale.

"Is it dishonorable to accept something for the pain?"

He forced a smile that was far from reassuring. "I hope whatever you have is strong."

I took one of my sleeping needles and discharged half the drug into a wad of cloth before injecting the rest into him.

"Will I sleep?"

"You'll feel very, very drunk," I replied. At least that was what the eunuchs had reported when we tested the serum.

Makoto nodded slowly. "That sounds good."

The more serious wound had to be sewn, but due to the drug or Makoto's warrior spirit, he made barely a sound as I threaded the needle over the wound. By the time I finished bandaging him, his eyelids were drooping. He murmured something as I closed his robe.

"What was that?"

He opened his eyes a fraction wider. "*Arigato.*"

I nodded, not sure I did anything more than make him look less cut up.

"I am not dying today, Lady Jin." His voice was starting to drift. "Someone else took my place." He nodded toward the far wall. "That should have been me."

Satomi sat near the door with her head bent as she worked on her rifle. Her hair fell over her face, hiding it. Takeda sat beside her, speaking in a quiet tone. The sword he'd taken from the fallen assassin lay beside him on the floor. If we were attacked again, the inventor was the only able-bodied warrior left among us.

I went next to Chang-wei, who sat with his back propped up against the wall.

"Let me see your arm."

He recoiled when I reached for him. "It's not bad."

With a sigh, I took hold of him and carefully unwrapped the makeshift bandage he'd created. The cut had taken him across the back of his forearm, missing the joint. The wound had mostly closed. It was hard to tell how deep it was—the katana were razor sharp. A thin red line could hide a wound that cut to the bone.

When I tried to pull up his sleeve to rebind the wound, Chang-wei jerked away, causing fresh blood to seep from the cut.

"Stupid!" I snapped.

It was poor of me to take my frustration out on him like that, but I was exhausted and still very frightened. And he *was* being stupid.

"I'm sorry," Chang-wei said, suitably chastised. "It was reflex."

Holding his wrist firmly, I pulled back his sleeve and saw the angry red line that traveled down his arm. I stared at it for half a minute before binding the minor cut.

"How long have you had this?" I asked, deadly quiet.

It looked like blood poisoning, which wasn't possible from today's injuries. My insides were a mix of emotions. If I could sort them out, the primary one would be anger. Then disbelief. But anger first.

"It's nothing."

"It's *not* nothing. And I'm getting tired of hearing that."

To a healer, that denial was far from helpful. I didn't raise my voice at him this time. Instead, I remained cold and calm.

"How long have you had this?" I repeated.

"I first saw it just two days ago."

The skin around the line felt hot. "What caused this infection?"

As far as I knew, Chang-wei hadn't suffered any recent

injuries aside from today's confrontation, but even the smallest cut could become infected.

"It's not an infection," he insisted. "Or not the sort you would think."

There was no use in arguing now, when I didn't have the herbs necessary to treat the condition. The airship had contained a cargo of medicinal herbs. When we returned to the Chinese quarter, I would hopefully find what I needed. I made a silent vow to keep watch on Chang-wei in the meantime.

"They're saying Lord Takeda is not the target," Chang-wei said, indicating the conversation near the door.

Takeda and Satomi both turned to us at once. "I offered myself," Takeda explained. "It wasn't an act of bravery, on my part. Merely etiquette. I thought the *hitokiri* would ignore the rest of you if they achieved their purpose."

"My father was struck down in a crowded schoolhouse," Satomi added. "No one else was harmed."

I didn't know what to say. To me, the samurai code seemed uncommonly brutal; to breathe was to die. Yet they hung the trappings of honor and civility over it.

"But the assassins would not accept those terms," Chang-wei pressed.

"They seemed to have another target in mind."

We all looked to Chang-wei. The *hitokiri* had paused over him. The rest of us were expendable, but the shogunate wanted Chang-wei alive.

A shudder ran through me. "We brought this upon you."

Takeda exhaled slowly. "This day has been coming for a long time. Satomi-san and I will take watch."

Satomi finished preparing her firearm and stood to accompany him.

"Lady Sagara," Chang-wei called out as she reached the storehouse door. "I'm sorry for the loss of your guardsman."

Satomi turned, her expression haunted.

"He was a loyal friend," he went on. "It was an honorable death."

She dipped her head briefly to acknowledge the tribute, though she had yet to shed a single tear for her companion.

"Yoshiro was only *karakuri*." She looked sadly to Takeda. "An illusion created from metal and wood. And yes, his was an honorable death."

17

K arakuri.

Like the puppets in the teahouse. The automatons in Takeda's workshop.

We traveled in silence over the next day, lying low whenever we could. Even though Yoshiro had been a machine, we felt his loss like the loss of a comrade. He had traveled with us for days, and I had never suspected. Though I'd never seen his face beyond the war mask, I had attributed a range of emotions to him. Concern, determination and even affection when he hovered over Satomi. All those moments took on an eerie cast now.

Nagasaki city grew nearer with each step, but we still had thousands of steps to go. We trudged through the small roads along the rice paddy terraces cut into the hills. The air was damp and the ground muddy beneath our feet.

I took Satomi's side as she guarded the rear. Lord Takeda took the front with Makoto and Chang-wei at the center. Makoto could only move slowly, but he continued without complaint. He had already offered to be left behind, but we had refused.

We were all in this together. My gaze darted along the terraces. The visibility was clear among these fields. Satomi and her rifle had the advantage over a swordsman with a katana. Firearms were weapons for a less civilized age marked by violence.

I expected the black shadows to fly at us at any moment.

Satomi had said nothing more about Yoshiro, which left me to ponder how he'd come about. Now that I looked back, all the peculiarities of his presence made sense. He'd never spoken, never eaten, never slept. He had also been impervious to pain.

"My father and Takeda-sama created him" was all Satomi would say about her mechanical bodyguard as we walked side by side.

The Japanese scientists had fused art and knowledge into one. For the first time, I realized the scope of Japanese technical advancements.

We all remained lookout as we made our way back to Nagasaki, city port of foreigners and outcasts. With every moment, we were prepared for battle to once again erupt around us.

I watched my charges as they trudged in front of me. Makoto moved with a slow gait, his weight shifted to nurse his injury. Despite the stiffness of his movements, his hand remained near his sword. No matter how injured he was, he would die with steel in his hands.

Chang-wei appeared steadier, but there was a pallor beneath his complexion. The rifle Satomi had granted him rested firmly in his hands.

What had happened to him? Had Yizhu had him drugged? Some form of slow-acting poison to ensure he'd return? Even with my work in the Court of Physicians, I only knew a fraction of the substances in the apothecary. The antidote must be lying there in some secret combination of drawers.

Chang-wei was confident he need only return to Peking to be cured, but I didn't trust them.

"Is there room on that airship for me?" Satomi asked.

She spoke in such a low tone that I nearly missed it.

"By order of the shogunate, a countryman who has left our shores can never return," she continued before I could reply. "But I killed a samurai. With a gun." She adjusted the strap on her shoulder. "Being a woman only compounds the crime. There's no place for me here any longer."

"Then you'll come with us," I promised.

Chang-wei turned his head partway back toward us before returning his focus ahead.

I didn't have the authority to offer Satomi passage, but we owed it to her. And I still had a feeling deep in my soul that we were connected by fate.

As to what awaited us in Peking when we returned with our unlikely companions, I couldn't say. At first it seemed as if danger had followed us to the island empire, but now I knew that the dark cloud of it was everywhere. Like a tangled net thrown over our heads. Grasping the end of the net were *Yingguo* and the Western nations while we fought and thrashed inside, fighting against ourselves instead of the true enemy.

WE STOPPED for rest among the terraced rice fields, begging food and drink for our midday meal from a nearby farmhouse. With Lord Takeda's noble demeanor, the peasants were obligated to comply.

I took the time to check Makoto's bandages.

"See, just a scratch," he boasted, back in his usual spirits. I refrained from telling him that the scratch had been dangerously close to spilling his guts out.

Chang-wei wasn't doing as well. The red line beneath his skin had traveled up past his elbow, and the fever had taken hold. He barely ate at all, drinking only a few sips of water while we rested. He kept his eyes closed as I felt for his pulse.

"They injected you with something," I said, barely containing my anger. "If you know what it was, I can try to counteract it."

He shook his head wearily. "The imperial court was just being cautious."

"So you wouldn't flee?"

"I know too many secrets." He opened his eyes to look at me. "Clever of them, really."

"This is uncalled for."

"As long as we return to Peking soon, I'll be fine."

I steeped dried chrysanthemum petals to treat the fever, but I doubted it was strong enough. Within the hour after we'd set out again, his steps were dragging. I took the rifle, which he relinquished without argument. Makoto wouldn't touch the firearm, and Takeda, despite his studies of Western advancements, declined the weapon as well. I kept it slung around my shoulder. It was surprisingly light.

By late afternoon, we could see the outlying hills of the port city.

"It will be easier to sneak back in at night though the same passage," Makoto suggested.

"I would like to visit my father's school one last time."

Satomi had hardly spoken for most of the day. There were no objections, so we planned to wait there until dark. After curfew had passed, there would be less of a guard presence around the Chinese quarter. The regular crew of Japanese laborers and entertainers would have left for the night.

We made it to the abandoned building in time to see the sun dipping over the edge of the cliffs just beyond. Wordlessly, Satomi slipped inside, and we allowed her privacy to pack whatever effects she wanted to take with her. The rest of us congregated around the workshop, the main study stained by Lord Sagara's final moments.

Takeda set his lantern down and drifted to the *elekiteru* box in the corner, just as Chang-wei had done days earlier. The two of them really were of one mind.

"You had a hand in building the clockwork samurai, didn't you?" Chang-wei asked.

"I made his body," the inventor admitted, with just the faintest hint of pride. "But Shintarō-san built his heart."

"How?"

Lord Takeda smiled sadly as he touched his hand to the wheel of the broken generator. "A *karakuri* maker is protective of his trade secrets. If everyone knew how his creations worked, then the illusion would be destroyed."

But the bodyguard had been more than an illusion. He had walked among us. He'd fought against trained warriors. I knew what Chang-wei was thinking.

"Mechanical soldiers," he said, barely able to contain his excitement. "Imagine the possibilities."

Takeda shook his head. "We thought the same once, but the *bakufu* opposes the replacement of swords with guns. Vulgar devices that take away any difference between a warrior and a peasant. Imagine what they would think of a creation that replaces a warrior completely with gears and wires."

It would be considered an abomination. "Such a thing would threaten the very core of the shogunate," I said.

"But we built it anyway."

Takeda set down the journal he'd carried all the way from his villa. Chang-wei looked at it with interest, but all we could see were the familiar yet unfamiliar characters of the Japanese script.

"How did you power it?" Chang-wei insisted. "A windup mechanism would have worn down quickly."

"That was Shintarō-san's secret to keep." The scientist bowed his head reverently. "A good friend."

Now Chang-wei had a problem to solve. "A generator contained inside the mechanism? But it would have to be small."

As I looked at the *elekiteru*, it came to me. Satomi had used a glove fitted with copper wires to send electricity into the *hitokiri*. Blue white lighting had crackled over the armored warrior, felling him.

"The energy is stored in container."

Takeda looked pleased. "A good thought."

Aside from his cryptic smile, he refused to reveal any more.

Both Chang-wei and I looked to the ceramic jars gathering dust in the corner. On first glance, they had looked like wine jugs. Still too big to have been contained inside Yoshiro's frame, but the idea was intriguing. Lightning in a jar.

It was Satomi who had the answers to Chang-wei's questions, not Lord Takeda. I remembered her kneeling before her body-guard with her hand to his chest. She had been checking his heart—or his energy store. I had mistaken it for a tender moment, though maybe it had been exactly that. The clockwork warrior had been her father's master creation.

"The *karakuri* took us years to build," Takeda explained. "We did it for art and for pride. Easier to train a soldier in terms of efficiency."

But I could see Chang-wei was thinking, laying out his own designs.

"*Shina-jin*, you should come see this."

Makoto called to us from the far window where the paper had mostly worn away. In the distance, I could see an orange light, brighter than the earlier sunset.

Chang-wei moved to the window, each step labored. His strength was fading. Despite that, he hurried outside a moment later. I rushed to follow him into the night air with Makoto and Lord Takeda immediately behind me.

"What is it?" I asked, alarmed.

He had rushed to the edge of the plateau, where we had a view of Nagasaki Bay as well as the port city. At the edge of the city lay the airfield where we had landed. Plumes of black smoke rose into the sky to disappear into the night.

Our airship was on fire.

18

"We have to get back to the Chinese quarter." Chang-wei returned to the schoolhouse to retrieve our packs and call for Satomi. There was no more time to waste.

"It could be a trap," Makoto argued.

"They'll be looking for us," Chang-wei agreed, but he didn't slow his pace.

I didn't know how long he could continue pushing like this. When I took hold of his arm, he was burning with fever.

"We need to think this over," I said in a low voice.

He looked at me, and I could see the redness in the rim of his eyes. "The shogunate is trying to strand us here. Any ally we have is within the walls of Chinese settlement."

They wanted Chang-wei. Somehow they knew an imperial engineer had come to their shores, and they wanted him under their control.

"We can try the Dutch," Takeda suggested. "Dejima Island is close to the Chinese quarter."

"And we'll have a fine time passing as Westerners," Makoto scoffed. "Better chances in the *Tōjin yashiki*. Let's go."

He muttered something about mad scientists as we started down the hillside. I took Chang-wei's side as we walked.

"There are . . . other ways . . . off the islands," he said, his breathing labored between each word.

"That isn't what I'm worried about." That wasn't entirely true, but there was something more urgent. "You're weakening quickly."

I could almost see the life draining from him. Whatever they had done was bleeding him dry.

"What did they give you? If you want my help, you need to tell me." I wasn't going to accept any more lies from him.

"It was . . . it was a measure to ensure my loyalty. A blood oath. They were trying to frighten me. I didn't believe anything would come of it."

My chest constricted. "What did they do?"

Chang-wei sighed, pressing a hand to his temples. "They summoned the grandmaster imperial physician."

I frowned. "There's no such person."

"Apparently the grandmaster lives as a recluse in one of the temples within the palace grounds. The man looked like he was at least a hundred years old."

He was right. It sounded more like myth than reality.

"He fixed five needles into what he claimed were forbidden points," Chang-wei continued. "I knew they were playing into superstitions and nothing more."

Forbidden points were mentioned in every acupuncture manual, though some were openly passed on and others merely hinted at. The premise was simple—just as acupuncture could heal, it could harm. Even kill. From these few words, many legends had spread of a death touch. A slight pressure at key points that could cause major injury or death.

Of course it sounded like groundless mysticism to a man of science such as Chang-wei.

"If I didn't return in ten days, the energy released from the forbidden points would stop my heart. It's nonsense."

The way he pressed his hand to his chest told me he wasn't so certain anymore.

"If this is all nonsense, then what's happening to you?" I demanded.

He sighed, shaking his head. "It's coincidence, Soling. We need to stay focused."

Chang-wei was stubborn, but he was also right. We needed to get to safety.

We stowed our weapons as we neared the city limits. Despite being injured, Makoto moved to the front. With him and Lord Takeda at the lead, we moved with purpose into Nagasaki. The streets only looked vaguely familiar to me. We had ventured out only once and at a much later hour.

This evening, the streets were filled with pedestrians. Lanterns hung by the doors, and the smell of sandalwood incense wafted into the street. It was only when I heard the chorus of female laughter that I realized where we were.

We were in the brothel district on the outskirts of town. Strategically, it made sense for smuggling routes to pass through there. No one questioned why there were new faces in the area or why they were gone the next day.

No one paid the colorful song girls and hostesses any mind, except for Satomi, who couldn't look away.

"Such could have been my fate," she told me.

It could have been mine as well. Wives and daughters from families that had fallen into disgrace often went to tea houses and brothels.

The airship still smoldered in the distance, visible only as a haze of smoke. None of the city dwellers paid it much mind beyond an occasional glance. What was happening in the Chinese quarter? Were the shogunate's agents searching every shop and drinking house now?

The distillery appeared as empty as it had when we'd left. Makoto opened the door. After a brief inspection, he ushered everyone inside and slid the wooden bolt in place behind us.

We wove through the maze of vats and pipes. Even though I'd been through it once before, I wouldn't have remembered how to get to the hidden passageway. Makoto opened a panel in the floor, which led down to the storeroom where we first entered.

Once we were all down below, Makoto lit several lanterns, handing one to Chang-wei and the other to Takeda.

"I'll go first. If I encounter any danger down there, I'll signal you. Run back as fast as you can."

"You've already done enough," Chang-wei told him. "There's no need for you to endanger yourself any further."

Makoto shook his head. "We are all in this together now. Besides, you would get hopelessly lost without me."

Chang-wei moved to help Makoto push aside the crates from the passageway. One by one, we crawled into the hole in the wall. On the other side, a large brick was shoved in place to seal the opening.

The first time we'd navigated these tunnels, it had been completely dark. Now, with the lanterns, I could see how extensive they were. A corridor passed through the entry point into the distillery. Makoto led us through, and as I walked in the maze, I wondered if there were other passageways throughout Nagasaki. There must have been. The tunnels split off at places, snaking away into parts unknown.

Finally we reached a dead end where a ladder had been propped up against the dirt wall.

"Is this our destination?" Lord Takeda asked.

Makoto nodded. His hand was pressed to his side. I prayed he hadn't reopened the wound. He wasn't the sort who would complain about it if he did. Makoto was the sort who would bleed to death, silent and stoic.

"I'll go first," Lord Takeda offered, not mentioning Makoto's injury. Satomi moved forward to hand him her pistol, but he waved it aside.

Chang-wei helped him set the ladder and held on to it to stabilize it as Lord Takeda climbed to the trapdoor. With some effort, he pushed it open, but he paused on the ladder with his face aboveground, hidden from view.

"What is it, Takeda-sama?" Satomi asked.

"Not good," came the muffled reply. "Not good."

Moments later, we all walked through the wreckage of the teahouse by the dim light of our lanterns. Shards of porcelain lay strewn over the floor. Lord Takeda stopped before the shattered frame of one of the tea-serving *karakuri*. The puppet lay sad and broken at his feet.

"This does not seem like the work of the *bakufu*," Takeda said gravely.

"The shogunate has certainly shown itself capable of violence," Chang-wei remarked.

I edged closer to him as a shudder traveled down my spine. The air itself felt oppressive. My instinct was to flee, but who knew what waited for us out in the quarter?

"I understand what Takeda-sama is saying," Satomi chimed in. "The samurai way is one of efficiency. Of swift justice. This—" She took in the rubble around us. "This was blind."

A sound came from the far wall, making us jump. Satomi spun around with her firearm raised, and Takeda and Makoto were quick to reach for their swords. Chang-wei shoved me behind him, shielding me with his body.

I heard the sound of a wooden door sliding open. "Are they gone?"

It was Yelu, the teahouse proprietor, crouched inside one of the service panels. Makoto lowered his arm to help him up.

"The authorities from the customs office came looking for you," he told Chang-wei, his voice trembling. "It was the opium. They found opium in your cargo hold."

Chang-wei and I exchanged a glance.

"There was no opium on that ship." I turned to our comrades. "We came here to seek an alliance."

"Perhaps your captain didn't have the same goal," Makoto replied coldly.

"This voyage was approved by the Grand Council," Chang-wei said. "They wouldn't have allowed opium into our hold."

"It wasn't opium," I cut in, the realization coming to me. "There was something more incriminating aboard the airship."

"The signal receiver." Chang-wei shook his head. "It was hidden, but—"

"But if the trade authorities found it, they would assume we were spies."

"Or scientists," Lord Takeda proposed. "The shogunate planted the opium so it could destroy your airship and keep you here in Nagasaki." He looked directly at Chang-wei. "Just as I am valuable to your Emperor, Engineer Chen is valuable to our shogunate. They wanted Engineer Chen. They may have even allowed you to leave the settlement and journey deeper into the countryside. Then none of your countrymen could witness your capture."

It was all becoming clear. "From the moment we set foot in Nagasaki, we were trapped."

By then we had all come to the same conclusion, but it was Chang-wei who spoke. "Someone acted as an informer."

THE PROPRIETOR SCURRIED from the teahouse as soon as he was convinced we wouldn't harm him. He had kept his part of the bargain well enough by not informing on us. Our party was left with the problem of what to do now that we were wanted criminals, each and every one of us.

"We can go back out through the tunnels," Makoto suggested. "Hide away in the countryside."

Chang-wei shook his head. "The only way out of Japan is through this port. We can't go back."

Though he fought to hold himself steady, sweat collected on his brow. The fever was burning through him.

"Without our airship, we're stranded." I tried to remain calm. "Will anyone allow us passage?"

"There's always someone willing to bend the rules for the right price." Chang-wei didn't look so certain.

There were only a handful of Chinese ships in the harbor, all captained by men who depended on Japanese trade for their livelihood.

"But there might be another way," Chang-wei continued. "A potential ally inside the settlement."

"Who?" I asked.

"As I said, he's a potential ally."

Which meant it was someone we couldn't trust.

Satomi finished checking her firearms while Takeda went to check the streets.

I turned to Makoto. "Your duty to us is done. It would be no dishonor to leave now."

"We finish this together," the swordsman said gravely.

"There isn't much time. The guard patrol might return." Chang-wei retrieved a folded map from his pocket and held it close to the lantern. "We need to go to the northwestern quarter."

A dark look passed over Makoto's face. "That is where the wealthiest *tojin* set up residence. Chinese traders," he replied at my puzzled expression.

I remembered seeing the spacious courtyards from overhead as we flew into the airfield.

"The streets are clear," Takeda reported.

Chang-wei directed him to the back of the group along with Satomi. Though Lord Takeda was a man of science, his grip on the *katana* spoke of more than a passing familiarity with the weapon as we prepared to venture out. Makoto begrudgingly took the center while I took Chang-wei's side at the head.

"How are you?" I asked beneath my breath.

"I'm fine." There was strain in his voice. Could stimulation of forbidden points really cause a man to waste away so quickly?

We spilled out from the teahouse into the dark alleys of the warehouse district. After a scan of the area, Chang-wei turned to the right.

"*Engineer Chen.*"

A voice called out in the darkness, and we all froze.

"Captain Zhao?"

Chang-wei kept the rifle hidden behind his back, but I watched his grip shift slightly as he prepared to swing it around if necessary. A dark figure moved through the lane, gradually taking form as he ventured closer to our lanterns.

"Where were you?" Zhao asked in a muted tone. "They took the ship."

"Why didn't they take you as well?" Chang-wei replied.

I didn't wait for an answer. Drawing my needle gun from my sash, I aimed and fired a needle into the side of his neck. Zhao looked confused at first, then he clawed aimlessly at the needle before crashing to the ground.

It had to be Zhao. He depended on Nagasaki for his livelihood and profited from being allowed to trade there. Sometime during his many visits to the island empire, his loyalties had shifted.

No one questioned my judgment. Instead we hurried on, stepping over the captain's sleeping form.

"The patrols could be close," Chang-wei said in a hushed voice.

He held a *gando* lantern with the metal shield around it adjusted to only allow a thin sliver of light. Enough to light our path but not direct the authorities to us. I prayed they were still searching near the market where we had rented rooms in one of the inns. That would keep them occupied at the opposite end of the settlement.

As we crept through the narrow lanes and alleyways, the dwellings grew considerably larger. Chang-wei came to a stop before a mansion with a red roof and dragon and phoenix ornaments. Ivy crawled over the surrounding walls.

"This place?" Makoto asked, incredulous.

I looked back at him. "You know it?"

"This *tojin* has a reputation. He captains a trading junk that can out sail any vessel on the sea. Rumor has it the customs office turns a blind eye to some of his activities."

"What exactly do you mean?" Satomi asked, irritated.

"They say he's a pirate."

Makoto knew more about the inhabitants of the Chinese quarter than he let on. I wanted to ask him more about that, but this wasn't the time or place. Unperturbed, Chang-wei pulled the bell string at the gate.

"Do you know him?" I asked Chang-wei as we waited.

"Once I did," he replied, keeping his gaze forward. "You may know him better now."

I didn't have long to ponder that answer. The gate opened to reveal a familiar face with its sharp cheekbones and angular features. His hair was cut short, ending just above his shoulder, and he was dressed in a long Western-style waistcoat that fell to his knees. The air drained from my lungs. The last time we'd seen Yang Hanzhu was during a battle between his ship and an imperial vessel at sea. Yang had willingly handed me his gunpowder formula before allowing me to escape.

"Chen Chang-wei." His acknowledged his former colleague, his smile stretched tight. When he turned to me, his look was noticeably warmer. "*Mèimèi*. Did you like the flowers?"

Chang-wei glanced briefly between us. He kept his tone neutral as he spoke. "How are you . . . Brother?"

There was a noticeable pause before the honorific. Perhaps

they had been like brothers once when they were both serving in the Ministry under my father, but according to Yang, they had never gotten along.

"You don't look well," Yang remarked, looking Chang-wei over from head to toe. "It would be best to continue the conversation inside. If you've come to me for help, then it must be a matter of life and death."

19

We were ushered through the front gate, and Yang closed the heavy door behind us.

The interior of the courtyard was built like a Chinese mansion one might find in the wealthy areas of Peking or Shanghai, but there were traces of Japanese influence in the rooftops and windows. I knew Yang Hanzhu came from wealth, but I didn't realize how much. Despite the opulent surroundings, the grounds were eerily empty. No lights glowed from within the chambers. No servants came to greet us.

"You know our situation," Chang-wei said as we followed Yang through the courtyard.

Yang looked him over, taking full measure of his former colleague. "I know your situation. However, I didn't expect such a gathering."

"Can you help get us out of Nagasaki?" I asked, stepping in. "All of us," I added as Yang looked thoughtfully at the other three.

"I sense your friends are are subjects the shogunate will not relinquish easily," he remarked. "Especially considering the recent news."

Lord Takeda had remained quiet up until that moment. "What news?"

"Reports have started coming in about the approach of a Western fleet. *Měiguó rén*. The Americans." The way Yang spoke the word had an ominous ring to it. "The captain has refused to dock at Nagasaki and is instead directing his fleet toward Edo." Just as the English devil ships had forced their way into our harbors nearly ten years ago.

"When?" Takeda demanded.

"Soon—" Yang cocked his head suddenly. "What is that sound?"

The whine of metal gears came from the other side of the wall, along with the rise and fall of armored feet.

"*Watch out—*"

The words barely left my lips before the assassin vaulted high over the wall, landing with a thud onto the stone courtyard. I had barely enough time to drag myself out of its path. A moment later a shot rang out—it had to be from Satomi. The bullet merely glanced off the *hitokiri's* steel chest plate.

Lord Takeda led the next attack, sword flashing. The assassin didn't need a weapon. It deflected the blade with its forearm, and sparks flew from the impact.

The cage of armor around the intruder enhanced his strength, but it slowed him down. Takeda circled and attacked only to be knocked back by a swipe of the *hitokiri's* arm. It was easy to think of the assassin as inhuman, encased as it was in metal. Only his eyes showed through the samurai mask. They fixed coldly onto Chang-wei.

Chang-wei swung his rifle up, leveling it at the *hitokiri's* head. A shot between the eyes was the only way to stop it. Before Chang-wei could fire, something smashed over the assassin's back.

Yang stood behind the intruder and hefted another ceramic

container resembling a wine jug. He smashed the second one against the assassin's helmet, spilling liquid over the armor.

The *hitokiri* shook off the impact and resumed its advance. A thick syrup dripped from the steel plates as I fumbled for my pistol. I wasn't accustomed to firearms the way Satomi was. With everything happening so fast, I hadn't thought to draw.

Chang-wei backed up against me, shielding me as he took aim. But the shot was unnecessary. With each step, the assassin slowed. The substance coating the armor hardened until the metal assembly creaked to a halt. The *hitokiri* was frozen. Two black eyes glared at us, trapped inside the suit.

The jugs must have contained some sort of resin that dripped into the joints and gears and coated the armor like glue.

"If we're going to go, it must be now," Yang urged.

Gears whirred as the *hitokiri* struggled against its bonds. I could smell machine smoke from the grinding of metal, and small cracks appeared on the surface of the hardened resin.

That thing was strong enough to break free and reinforcements would be coming soon. We left the assassin in his cage and fled.

We raced toward the north end of the quarter. The armed patrol charged after us with a *hitokiri* at the lead, a comrade of the one Yang had disabled. My lungs burned, but I didn't dare slow to catch a breath.

"How . . . are we . . . going to get over?" I panted.

The settlement wall loomed ahead, rising nearly ten meters. I could sense Chang-wei close behind me. Makoto and Lord Takeda were just behind him.

Yang was unfazed. "We're not going over. We're going through."

I had no time to ask how we were going to get through the

thick slab of brick and mortar. Out of the corner of my eye, I saw Satomi coming to a halt to swing around.

"Keep going!" she shouted. "I'll hold them."

Her first shot cracked through the air and struck the *hitokiri* squarely in the chest, sending him reeling into the patrol men behind him.

I reached over to drag her along when an explosion shattered the air. The ground shook beneath our feet, and I fell to my knees, covering my head out of instinct. Another explosion followed before the echoes of the first one had faded.

Someone draped himself over me, holding me by the shoulders as he shielded me with his body. Chang-wei tried to say something, but I couldn't hear over the roaring in my ears. Wincing, I stayed down as pellets of gravel and stone rained down on us. When I looked up, I could see through to the harbor beyond.

Yang was the first on his feet. Chang-wei pulled me up, and even though my knees were shaking, I started running. I hoped the others followed us. It was hard to tell, because as soon as we passed through the opening in the wall, a thick fog surrounded us. It seemed to be rising off the water.

"Follow me."

It was Yang again. I held on to Chang-wei's arm as we stumbled through the mist. The explosion left me disoriented, but I thought Satomi was just behind us.

The mist had to be Yang's work. He had employed a similar diversion to escape at sea once. Some mix of chemicals dumped into the water to form the fog.

The murky outline of a trading junk loomed up ahead with its battened sails. Once more, we broke out in a run.

The gangplank was already lowered when we reached the pier. The gunpowder engine rumbled beneath the water. Yang was the first up into his ship. Makoto had a hand pressed to his wound, and Satomi took his arm to assist him up the plank.

I looked over my shoulder as I started to climb. Chang-wei remained on the dock, rifle positioned and ready to shoot.

The final figure through the fog was Lord Takeda. He held his sword in one hand but drew a book from the front of his robe with the other. Warrior and scholar.

"Take this." He handed the book to Chang-wei. "For Satomi."

She and Makoto paused on the gangplank as she turned to look back at him.

"It was your father's. Written in his blood." Lord Takeda then bowed to her and then Chang-wei. "I must take my leave now, friends."

"What will you do?" Chang-wei asked him.

"Surrender myself to the shogunate. The *bakufu* will need me in the days to come."

With the coming of the American fleet.

Takeda looked up once more to Satomi, and their eyes met. "Sayonara."

"Sayonara, Takeda-sama."

He turned to disappear into the mist, with his shoulders back and head high.

"Time to go," Yang called to us.

We resumed our climb. Chang-wei was the last on board, and Yang shouted the order to fire the engines. The crew hurried to raise the gangplank, and the low rumble of the engine became a roar. The ship was underway.

"But they might kill him," I said to Chang-wei.

"They might." Chang-wei looked down at the book in his hands. "But Lord Takeda was not willing to renounce his homeland. Not in its time of need."

"Country first," I intoned.

Chang-wei didn't answer.

The boom from the guard tower reminded us we weren't done yet. The ship cut through the bay as cannon fire landed in the water just off the port bow. The fog provided cover, but it was also a two-edged sword. We were moving fast and blind. One wrong turn and the ship could run aground.

Yang moved to the helm to steer as a whistling sound rose above us. The explosion this time came from on high, and the sky ignited in a blossom of yellow sparks.

Chang-wei swore. "They can see us."

A moment later, cannon fire crashed through the rear deck. We ducked as splinters flew everywhere.

"Get below deck!" Yang snapped.

Another whistle and pop ignited the sky with fireworks. I ran to the stairs and ushered Makoto and Satomi down first. Chang-wei was close behind as the tower cannon boomed. For a second, I prayed for a miss, but the junk shuddered violently with the impact.

Chang-wei had just cleared the top steps, but he lost his footing and stumbled into me. We held on to each other, righting ourselves just as a second engine roared to life. The ship jolted forward, and I listened, breath held, as the next volley of cannon fire fell wide.

We waited silently as the engines sped on. My heart pounded frantically until the cannons quieted. A sigh of relief ran through each of us—until we heard the sound of leaking water coming from somewhere down below.

20

Over the next few hours, the ship's carpenter plugged the hole and we were headed out of Nagasaki Bay.

"There aren't any ships in pursuit, but we're keeping watch," Yang reported. He only spoke with us briefly before going to join his crew. He still needed to steer his ship clear of danger.

Yang had had his crew at the ready as well as a route laid out for our escape. He had known we would come to him.

"We owe him our lives," I told Chang-wei.

Chang-wei appeared less than grateful to be in Yang Hanzhu's debt.

Our ragged party retired to the sleeping berths down in the hold. The escapes and battles of the previous days had bound the four of us together. Lord Takeda's absence left a palpable emptiness.

"Takeda-sama will be fine," Satomi murmured. "He made his choice."

And she made hers.

I felt the last of my energy drain from me. Only sheer will kept me on my feet.

"I should check the binding," I told Makoto.

He appeared similarly drained and didn't protest as I bent to tend to him. Chang-wei sank down in the opposite bunk as I pulled the edge of Makoto's robe aside. Blood seeped through the makeshift bandage. The wound appeared to have reopened during our escape.

"It's not bad," Makoto insisted in samurai fashion.

I hoped it was true. "I'll rebind it."

Last time I had sailed with Yang, they had no physician, but perhaps someone in the crew would know more about treating wounds than I did. They had to tend to their own injuries while at sea. All hands were busy at the moment.

Makoto exhaled and inhaled while I worked, steadying his breath to control the pain.

"I didn't expect you would come with us," I said. The conversation was in part a ploy to distract him.

"It was fate." Exhale. Inhale.

"We can try to smuggle you back through another location," Chang-wei suggested.

The swordsman closed his eyes, leaning his head back against the wall. "Nothing left for me there. I was disgraced and cast out of my clan."

I remained silent, merely focusing on the bandages. There was something about illness or injury that made one vulnerable. I was used to people confessing their secrets to me when I treated them.

"There was a merchant's daughter. Chinese. Beautiful." He let out a deep breath. "But it wasn't permitted, so I was stripped of my rank and exiled. And she . . . Her family's ship sailed and hasn't returned. I've waited for it, finding work among the *tojin* when I could, but now I know it was merely a fool's hope."

He turned to look at Satomi. "Your servant sacrificed himself to save my life. For that I owe."

Satomi didn't protest that Yoshiro had merely been an

automaton. Instead, she bowed her head to accept Makoto's offer graciously.

"We have no country any longer," she said quietly. "We are both outcasts."

Chang-wei reached into his robe and pulled out the book Takeda had handed him. "This is for you."

"Written in my father's blood." Satomi kept her expression neutral as she opened the first part. The characters were inscribed with black ink, but Takeda had meant Lord Sagara's life blood, his soul.

"For another time," Satomi said quietly, closing the book.

She set her rifle down beside her, then lay down with the book tucked against her arm like a child's doll. She promptly fell asleep like that, with her father's words near her heart. I prayed she would find some comfort in them.

"You should rest as well," I told Makoto. "Try not to disturb the binding."

"*Arigato*." With his sword tucked beneath his folded arms, he closed his eyes.

Chang-wei placed a hand on my shoulder, and for a moment I let myself soak in the stillness, with his touch anchoring me. We were safe, and we were together.

He started to recline back in his bunk, but I took him by the hand instead. His skin was hot to the touch, but his grip was firm as he held on to me. He regarded me with a question in his eyes as I led him away.

It had been a year since I'd been on the ship, but the layout came back to me easily. I found my way to the compartment that served as Yang's laboratory. The door was unlocked, and I led Chang-wei inside before lighting the lanterns.

He stared at the long tables and the various glass receptacles and apparatuses bolted to the surface. "What has he been doing here?"

"Experiments." I thought of the cabinets filled with chemicals and samples in the storeroom. One drawer had contained vials of blood. "Experiments on opium."

I know the scientist in Chang-wei wanted to explore the room, but that wasn't why I'd brought him here.

"Show me what they did to you." I feared the answer even as I led him to a chair.

Chang-wei hesitated but finally let out sigh, resigned. "Two points at the wrists."

I pulled back his sleeves, one side and then the other. The red line traveling up his arm had become more pronounced and visible on both sides.

"Two on either side of my torso."

"Show me."

He loosened his sash to open the front of his robe. Then he pulled the undershirt down. Acupuncture rarely left any visible mark, but I could see two inflamed points on his chest. I pressed my fingers against each site. The skin felt hot beneath them.

"And the final point?"

I tried to remain as calm as possible as he tapped a point immediately over his heart. The middle *dantian*, an energy point where qi gathered. That, in itself, meant nothing. The points themselves meant nothing. One had to know how to needle each point to stimulate it. Pressure, depth, all these nuances were significant.

"I wonder about the real reason Aguda sent you, Soling."

"You mean to spy on you?"

"Maybe he was trying to help me." His breathing was labored as he looked up at me. "Maybe he knew you could help."

I felt sick to my stomach. "I can't. I don't know anything about forbidden points."

I had only been practicing acupuncture for the last four years, and most of that as Physician Lo's apprentice. But Chang-wei no longer spoke as if he doubted what they'd done to him. And he regarded me with such trust in his eyes.

"The needles can't take away disease any more than they can inject them," I explained. "All I can try to do is right an imbalance. Restore the flow of energy where it's blocked."

Chang-wei smiled faintly. "Then right my imbalances."

He rose to remove his outer robe while I cleared away one of the laboratory tables. It would have to do. When I turned back around, Chang-wei had taken off his shirt, leaving his chest bare. His body was young and strong, tight with muscle that was usually hidden beneath scholars' robes.

I'd seen him once before like this, and just like that time, my cheeks heated. He stood watching me without a trace of shame. By all appearances, Chang-wei should have been at the height of health, not wasting away.

"Come lie on the table." My throat was dry when I tried to speak. "It's best if you can relax."

His eyes never left me as he came forward. I had seen other patients in such a state of undress when treating them, but this was Chang-wei. The man I had once thought would be mine.

Instead of climbing onto the table, he reached for me, his palm cradling my cheek.

"It's always like this, isn't it? You and me." His voice dropped low and deep, making my heart race. "And it always will be."

He tilted his head and leaned toward me, but I flinched away.

"Don't you dare," I said through my teeth. The corners of my eyes stung, and my anger was the only thing keeping the tears from falling. "If you care for me, then show it when you're not facing death. When you haven't been pushed to the edge of a cliff."

His lips were so close I could practically feel them pressed against mine, but he halted as I'd asked.

"This won't be death for me," he insisted. "The imperial court is trying to intimidate me, that's all."

Then why the fever? Why the lines indicating blood poisoning, and the drain of energy from his body? I broke away from his hold, and Chang-wei obediently climbed onto the lab table. It took some effort and he was out of breath by the end, but he made it on his own strength. That was important to see.

The mind will heal the body, Physician Lo had been fond of saying. My mentor was no man of great learning. He was a country doctor, and I, his assistant, but I thought of the truth of those words now.

"Breathe steadily," I instructed, placing my hand over his heart. I didn't do it for any diagnostic purposes. I just wanted to feel his heartbeat and know that he was still here. He was still alive, and I could help him.

I concentrated on my breathing as well, allowing the rhythm to center me. When I was ready, I reached for the leather folding case attached to my belt. There was only a limited set of needles there, but they would have to do. After another cleansing breath, I set to work.

Focusing my attention on Chang-wei instead of on my own fears helped calm me. I set the first needle at a point at the end of the heart meridian, which traveled from the hand up to the shoulder. Whatever the grand physician had done had disrupted the energy flow to Chang-wei's heart. I needed to try to restore it. Balance.

The points were grouped closely at the wrist. I fixed the needles one after the other, holding my breath. Only when I had moved to the next point near the elbow did I speak.

"When I came with you to Peking, I thought you had the Emperor's ear. That he was on your side."

Chang-wei's eyes remained closed, his breathing deep. "I do have his ear."

I had to bite back my anger. "But he allowed them to do this to you."

"There are many opposing forces within the court. The Emperor has to answer to all of them."

"He's the Emperor," I retorted. "His will is law."

"You know that's not true. Our all-powerful sovereign is far from all-powerful."

I fell silent, concentrating on the acupuncture points. The closer Chang-wei and I became, the further apart I realized we were. Could someone truly be that loyal? That self-sacrificing?

"Even if I managed to heal you, you would still return to the Ministry, to the imperial court, wouldn't you?"

His eyes were open now. "I must. The empire needs us, Soling."

He'd used this argument on me before. "They'll never trust you."

"They will when we win."

I continued the treatment along the heart meridian first on one side and then the other, hoping that I was restoring the natural flow of qi. Encouraging his body to right itself and fight off the disruption the imperial court had forced upon him.

Chang-wei fell asleep, and even though I was done, I stood and watched the steady rise and fall of his chest. His breathing seemed less labored now, the tension in his face relaxed. He was still feverish, but sleep would combat that. I wanted to believe he was healing.

What he was fighting for went beyond Emperor Yizhu and the imperial court. Chang-wei believed in preserving our land, our roots. Some small part of me understood it, but I could never be so trusting. I'd lost too much.

Half an hour passed before I finally woke him. Yang had cut the engines and allowed the ship to sail along, which must have meant we were out on the open sea and out of danger—for now.

Chang-wei seemed to lean more heavily on me as we walked together back to our berths. Whether it was because he meant to press closer to me or he needed the support, I didn't know.

∾

THE NEXT MORNING, we all watched the surrounding seas vigilantly for Japanese ships. There were none as the junk sailed clear of Nagasaki Bay and headed for open water. Once we were out of cannon range, the authorities seemed to have lost interest. Or perhaps they had recovered Lord Takeda. I prayed that he wasn't in chains this very moment. I prayed that he would be able to plead his case to the shogunate.

Makoto stood at the stern looking back toward shore long after it disappeared from view. In contrast, Satomi spent no time looking back. She absorbed herself in the rigging and the operation of the sails. I saw her watching the crew at work, her hair flying loose from its braid to whip around her face.

I treated Chang-wei once more in the morning with my needles. He was no better, but no worse, so I told him to get some rest. Regardless, I came to the upper deck midday to see him standing beside Yang, deep in conversation.

The two of them couldn't be more mismatched. Chang-wei's hair was pulled back into a traditional queue. The length of it formed a collar around his neck, and he still wore a Japanese robe. His shoulders were set back, and his spine was straight. Formal. Dignified.

Yang stood with a hand in the pocket of his waistcoat. His hair was cut short, the ends curling just above his shoulder. To a Westerner, he might have looked like a merchant or a gentleman, but in Peking, he couldn't be mistaken for anything but a rebel. A *hanjian*, to be specific. Race traitor and Western sympathizer. But he was neither of those. The imperial government had forced him out.

This was the first time the two of them had spoken in years, perhaps since my father's death. I waited for some argument to erupt, but they remained civil. Neither one so much as batted an eye.

I approached Yang much later when the sun was setting. He

stood alone at the bow. A plume of smoke rose above him to be picked up by the breeze.

"*Mèimèi.*"

He took one final pull from his cigarette before grinding it out against the side of a silver holding case. For the moment, he still appeared lost in thought.

"You spoke with Chang-wei?" I asked.

He gave a shrug as he tucked the case into a pocket in his jacket. "Of course I did."

"What did he say?"

"Same as always. Old times. Our golden days at the academy," he replied dryly.

It was well-known that the two of them were the youngest members of the Ministry when my father was at the head. Yang Hanzhu had passed the imperial science examinations on his first try at the age of eighteen. It was a feat that was unheard of until Chang-wei did the same several years later. Shortly afterward, my father had arranged my marriage to Chang-wei, though I had only been ten years old at the time. Plenty of time for him to establish a career in the imperial government before our actual wedding.

"It was mostly business. A stiff expression of gratitude for my assistance. How I was to return the two of you to your precious imperial court waiting in Peking. The same court that turned their back on you while you were in Japan, yet feels no reservation making use of the information you gained."

I knew better than to take his bait. "I'm grateful as well."

"What you really want to know is did Chang-wei talk about you?" Yang turned back to the water as if it were of no consequence. "He did."

My pulse jumped through no doing of my own.

"Perhaps the most interesting part of this conversation," he went on, "is how you've chosen to ask me about this rather than speaking to your intended yourself."

"He's not my intended—"

"I may not give you the answers you want, but you can trust me to be honest," he went on. "Chen Chang-wei is and has always been full of secrets."

I wanted to deny it in Chang-wei's defense, but I feared Yang would see the truth in my eyes.

"I'm surprised the honorable Engineer Chen didn't do what was right and make you his wife as he had promised." The corner of his mouth curled. "I thought that was what your future held when you chose him so dramatically—flying over the ocean."

I folded my arms over my chest. "I wasn't choosing Chang-wei."

He cocked his head. "You weren't?"

"I was choosing my family and the future of the empire."

"And I'm sure the empire is exactly why Engineer Chen refrains from acting on his desires. It'll always be duty first with him, even when it makes no rational sense."

I wasn't so certain of Chang-wei's unquestioning loyalty toward the Emperor any longer. Surely he could see how expendable we were to Yizhu.

"What is it between the two of you?" I asked.

"We disagree," he said simply. "On everything."

There was no use arguing with him. The two of them were very different down to their bones. Yang was all about taking action, while men like Chang-wei and Lord Takeda were skilled in biding their time. In building their defenses and bending more powerful forces gradually to their will, like a slow stream cutting through rock bit by bit to form a river.

What other options were there? Rebellion? Exile, as Yang had chosen? Or defeat and surrender? Certainly not.

"Will you return us to Peking?" I asked. When he didn't answer, my stomach knotted. We were on his ship and at his mercy.

"We have to return," I insisted. "You may not be able to tell, but Chang-wei isn't well."

"Anyone can tell." Yang turned back to the ocean, staring down into the waves. "I will return you to Peking, if that's what you wish. But he's blind, Soling. You have to realize that. He's blind and you are not."

21

"I won't be going with you to Peking," Satomi confided to me on merely the second day of the voyage. We were alone in the sleeping area. Makoto and Chang-wei had gone above deck for sunshine and fresh air.

"What about Makoto?" I asked.

She sat down beside me. "That scoundrel goes where he wants."

"He's all but pledged to protect you," I pointed out.

"Then he won't go to Peking, either."

Satomi had accepted his oath of loyalty without blinking. Though they had both given up name and country to go into exile, the class lines between them hadn't been erased. Satomi was noble-born, while Makoto had been of a lower class, serving his daimyo in hopes of rising in the ranks. Until he'd fallen in love.

"Perhaps that's best," I admitted.

They would have been outsiders in the imperial capital, or worse. Satomi would be exploited for her gun-making techniques and interrogated about her father's secrets.

"What will you do?" I asked her.

"Yang Hanzhu has agreed to let me stay on board as long as I take on a share of the work."

"As part of his crew?" I was surprised Yang would ask that of her, but then I realized it was likely Satomi who had come up with the offer. She was the one who had taken the steps to learn about the ship and its operation.

A woman couldn't live under a man's care without some sort of unspoken arrangement assumed, could she? Better to take control of her own life.

"I'll miss you," I confessed. She knew the pain I'd faced losing a father and having the responsibilities of the world suddenly on your shoulders.

Satomi smiled crookedly, but it quickly faded. "There's something I wanted to tell you."

She reached into a crevice on the side of her bunk and pulled out the book Chang-wei had given to her. It was folded in accordion style, with the pages formed out of one continuous sheet.

"I've been reading my father's words." She hesitated, turning through the pages one by one. "I think I know why Takeda-sama kept this book hidden. My father argues for adopting new methods, new ways of thinking."

"Western ways."

Satomi looked downward. "He criticizes the empires of China and Japan for harkening back to philosophies that are over a thousand years old. *The Art of War*. These ideas alone were enough to condemn him."

I could see how difficult it was for her to speak of this aloud. "My father was executed for declaring that our defenses were inferior and that we should study the ways of the *Yingguoren*."

"They shared similar ideas," Satomi said, opening to a page she had marked with a thread. "Father proposes that in order to protect the empire, one must go against the wishes of the *bakufu* if one knows their direction is wrong. He calls for a formation of a group of operatives, specially trained and educated, ranked by merit rather than nobility. The group would span professions and kingdoms."

My throat was suddenly dry. "A group that would act against the government if needed. Is there any mention of whether they formed such a group?"

Satomi shook her head. "It was only mentioned once."

Enough to constitute treason. Had our fathers communicated their arguments across the signal towers? I had always assumed my father was executed as an innocent. That he'd been loyal to the empire to his very last breath.

But if he had argued for rebellion. If he had secretly recruited others—

It was no wonder the imperial court had condemned the disciples closest to him. Many of them had been accused and put to death as well, leaving Kuo Lishen and an almost entirely new Ministry of Science.

My father had fought so hard for the Emperor. He'd taken the empire's failure onto his own head. That was the man I remembered, but I was learning that nothing was black-and-white. Not a subject's loyalty to his country—not even a daughter's memory of her father.

The moment of reflection didn't last long. There was some commotion overhead, and someone shouted my name. Satomi and I glanced at each other before I shot to my feet and rushed for the stairs.

The glare of the sun blinded me as a climbed above deck. Squinting, I saw the crewman circled on the far side. Yang was already there, parting the crowd and sending his men back to their posts.

Someone had fallen, and I knew, I knew what had happened before I saw him. With my heart in my throat, I ran to Chang-wei's side. Makoto was trying to rouse him but moved aside as I knelt down.

"He collapsed with no warning," Makoto reported. "I thought the sun—"

"It's not the sun." My words came out sharper than I intended, but there was no time for niceties. Chang-wei's complexion was frightfully pale. I felt for a pulse at his neck.

Nothing.

But he seemed to be getting better. He seemed stronger that morning—

My world tilted sideways. There was no time to cry. There was no time to wonder why. I pressed my ear to his chest, straining to hear a heartbeat.

Nothing. Nothing. Nothing.

"His heart isn't beating."

Makoto bowed his head. Above me, Yang stood silent. Even though he and Chang-wei had not gotten along, he placed a consolatory hand on my shoulder.

I wasn't ready to give up. "He's not dead. The flow of qi to his heart has been blocked," I explained, on the edge of desperation. "I have to restore the flow of energy."

This was unnatural. This was an intrusion forced upon a body that was still strong and healthy. I had to reverse it.

My mind was racing. Qi energy was tied intricately to breath and pulse. The acupuncture needles in my belt—they were used to guide the body back into its rightful rhythm, but they couldn't urge a heart to start beating again.

I hadn't noticed Satomi had left until she came back above deck, running toward me. In her hand was a mass of copper wire.

She knelt on the opposite side of Chang-wei. The device in her hands was the glove from the night of the first *hitokiri* attack. She tore away the glove, leaving behind what looked like a metal disc with a dial on top. Two sets of wires hung from it.

She shoved it into my hands. "Can you use this?"

Her words seemed to come from far away. I realized what she had handed me was a container. My head pounded as I recalled the cage of blue light surrounding the *hitokiri*.

Lightning in a jar.

"This will kill him," I protested.

"He's dying now."

The next moments came in flashes. I stared at Satomi. At Chang-wei.

It was all there, connected. Qi. Electricity. Diagrams of internal organs. Yoshiro with an automaton's body and an electric heart.

I dragged open Chang-wei's robe. His skin was still warm. My needles were in my hands. Two points. I forced my mind to focus. Two points, with energy lines that passed through the heart. Direct the flow.

In the next moment the needles were in place. I attached the wires with steady hands. I could tremble later. I could doubt myself later.

As I placed my hand on the dial, I met Satomi's eyes. She wasn't certain. I wasn't certain, either.

I turned the dial halfway, and nothing happened. So I cranked it all the way.

Chang-wei's frame jumped upon the deck, his back arching as the electricity flowed through him. Quickly I turned back the dial. The world held still as I lowered my head to his chest. Even the ocean waves seemed to have halted their sway.

Within this stillness, I felt the beat of his heart against my cheek.

"Don't do that again," I commanded, choking back tears. Chang-wei hadn't yet regained consciousness. I held on to him a little longer, listening to the steady rhythm of his heartbeat in my ear.

~

I WAS LYING beside Chang-wei when he awoke later that day. He reached out to touch my hair first before saying anything.

"Where am I?" His voice sounded scratchy, as if he'd been unconscious for a long time rather than a few hours.

"The captain's quarters."

It was the largest cabin on the ship and the most private. Chang-wei glanced about, trying to orient himself, before returning his gaze to me. His fingers curled into my hair. "Thank you."

He couldn't have known what had happened. Maybe I would explain it all to him later once I had time to clear it up in my own mind, but for now he was looking at me as if I was the only thing in the world.

I didn't say anything, merely moved closer so I could curl up against him. His arms wrapped around me, holding on tight.

~

THE ESCAPE from Nagasaki had taken us off course. According to Yang, the situation in Shanghai had become too unstable to hazard a landing. I tried to ask more about that, but all he knew was that the shipping lines had been disrupted and there was news of unrest. Ningpo, a treaty port north of Shanghai we had also surrendered to the *Yangguizi*, would have to do.

The journey home would take us four days by Yang's estimation, and we all settled in as best we could.

Chang-wei recovered steadily. After the surge of energy through his heart, the obstruction the grand physician had injected seemed to have cleared. His pulse recovered its natural rhythm, but I still kept careful watch, searching for any lingering signs of illness. Within a day, Chang-wei was well enough to even venture down into the engine room to speak to

Old Liu Yentai, the ship's engine master. They had both been colleagues in the engineering corps of the Ministry under my father.

I found Satomi exploring the deck in the mornings, speaking with the crew. She even had Yang's ear at times. His demeanor was all seriousness as he pointed out some part of the rigging to her.

The third day found us all on deck, enjoying the sun. The shore was not yet visible, but I sensed the promise that it was there. At times like this, when the ship became the entirety of our world, I felt both large and small at once. Chang-wei was reclined against the quarterdeck, sketching in a notebook. I sat down beside him and peered over his shoulder.

It was a drawing of a swordsman fitted with the steel cage armor of the *hitokiri*.

"We can integrate the mechanical parts with nerve impulses using acupuncture needles," he proposed. "The suits would be more maneuverable. Less clumsy."

The acupuncture biomechanics used to aid lost or broken limbs had never been employed on a large scale. Integrating a full suit to enhance a body's strength and speed had never been heard of.

"It's possible," I said, maintaining a cautious stance.

"Between the automatons and the rifle designs. Electricity experiments. If we could have come to an agreement with Japan, it could have turned the entire war."

Each of our nations had its own concerns and its own directives. We were not of one mind, and we never would be, as much as Chang-wei might hope it. It couldn't be helped.

Had Lord Takeda persuaded the shogunate to prepare for the Western invasion? Was he in chains now? Somehow, I knew in my heart he would be able to come to an understanding. They needed him, and they knew it. It was a precarious position that I knew too well—to be valuable and dangerous at once.

"I would have liked to know more about the lightning cylinder," Chang-wei confessed.

The container had been one of Lord Sagara's inventions. Satomi had only a passing knowledge of how it worked, and our last use of it seemed to have depleted its store.

He turned the page and then quickly turned to the next, but not before I caught a glimpse of what had been there.

"What was that?"

"Nothing—"

He tried to use his shoulder to block me, but I grabbed the corner of the page and flipped it back.

"Is that a drawing of me?" It was half accusation, half question. My heart thudded in a giddy rhythm.

"Of course not."

I couldn't help smiling.

"It's a design for a *karakuri*. She dances and sings. She does whatever I want."

I jabbed him with my elbow. He grinned at me, and I made a face back before falling silent. Too much had happened to pretend we could tease each other without a care. We'd never had that freedom between us.

"You don't really look like that," he said after a pause.

"Oh?"

Chang-wei closed the notebook and ran a nervous hand over the cover. His look was both serious and earnest. "You're prettier than that. I mean, I'm better at drawing technical diagrams than faces."

"Can I see it again?"

"Not yet. Maybe when she's finished."

The drawing hadn't been hideous by any means. If anything, it was flattering. I didn't taunt Chang-wei further. In two days, he'd both admitted he wanted to marry me—though without actually proposing—and he'd admitted he thought I was pretty. I looked out at the endless blue on blue. We were headed back to the mainland and then home, but maybe I didn't mind being out to sea so much.

He followed behind me as I retired below, but when we reached the foot of stairs, I felt his hand on my arm, turning me around. We were tucked beneath the stairwell, with me in his arms.

"What are you doing?"

The corner of Chang-wei's mouth twitched. "I'm doing as I'm told."

He kissed me then, holding me against him while the waves rolled beneath us.

At first I was afraid for him, but his heart beat strong against where we were pressed together. He took my face in his hands as he deepened the kiss. There was nothing for me to do but fall into it.

His mouth pressed against mine, not with enough force to frighten me, but hard enough for me to know that he'd wanted to do this for a long, long time.

"I'm not on the brink of death," he said huskily, breaking the kiss to sink a hand into my hair. "And I do care for you."

I remembered our first kiss, our only. And I had been waiting for our second every moment we were together. There were times over the last year I was in near tears, thinking it would never happen. But Chang-wei was here now, taking my mouth with a hunger that made my knees week. I held on to him and returned the kiss with the same feverish hunger.

"I want all of this," he confessed, pausing only for a moment before closing his mouth over mine once more. "I want a life with you. To marry you, as we had intended."

It was a long time before we pulled apart. But even then, his arms remained around me. He rested his cheek against my forehead while I tried to catch my breath.

"But I'm in constant danger, Soling. The imperial court

doesn't trust me. It never will. I can't tie you to my fate when my future is so uncertain."

"The danger will never go away," I told him. "And not because of this impending war with the West or because of the politics of the imperial court. It will never go away because you are Chen Chang-wei. You are who you are."

He reached out to run his thumb over my cheek. "Soling, I know you think I'm like Lord Takeda. Country before family, public before private. I know there are things I should have told you. For a long time now."

I was afraid that if I said something, he'd veer off course. So I remained as quiet and still as I could, willing him to continue.

"These are dangerous times, and I've committed to this path."

Now I couldn't remain silent. "I have as well," I told him, annoyed.

"I know you have. I know it even more now."

He reached for me in the tiniest of movements. His hand upon my elbow, drawing me closer more from will than physical touch.

"I told you before I guessed why Aguda had sent you with me."

I knew now, too. "Because of Yang Hanzhu. If you needed him, he would be more likely to help you with me by your side."

"Not only that," he denied, his tone fierce. "It's easy to get lost in a cause, to sacrifice yourself needlessly. He wanted someone to remind me why it was all important in the first place. Someone to bring me back."

I could barely breathe. "You need me," I told him fiercely.

Chang-wei smiled, one of his rare, genuine smiles that made my heart melt. "I do need you."

Before I could reply, we were interrupted by a creak of the stairs. We pulled apart quickly while Yang Hanzhu took one deliberately heavy step after another.

"I apologize for the intrusion," he said blandly, walking past us. He spared Chang-wei one pointed look before heading down the corridor. Together we stared at his back as he retreated.

When Chang-wei looked back at me, the moment was broken. But he was still breathing hard, his eyes bright and color high on his cheeks. He looked happy, as if there were no other place in the world where he could fit like this. And I felt the same. I felt it in my heart. This was part of the connection between us, and it could never be completely broken.

22

The door to Yang's laboratory wasn't locked. I was correct in guessing I would find him in there. He stood by one of the lab tables wearing a thick pair of gloves. Before him was Satomi's electrical cell. He had managed to remove the center panel and was scraping some of the residue from inside.

"What is in there?"

Yang remained focused on his work. "A mixture of salt and acid. There are multiple compartments surrounding the main chamber. They're all fitted with some confounded machinery."

Yang's focus was alchemical. Mechanical principles eluded him. I should have known that Yang or Chang-wei would fall over himself to dissect Lord Sagara's invention.

"I recognized the name Sagara immediately. Struck down in daylight, without a single protest. Such a waste," he spat. "A waste of a great mind. The same thing will happen to Chang-wei if he stays around the nest of ignorance that is the Forbidden City. Just think of the name. The place is closed off and isolated by design. Yet its inhabitants command the entire empire."

"At least Chang-wei believes in something," I argued.

"I believe in something," Yang insisted. He squared his shoulders while I waited, a look of challenge in my eyes. He only spoke one word.

"Peking."

I frowned at him, but a moment later I remembered his singular focus, the one reason he'd built this laboratory. "What's in Peking?"

"I've traced the tainted opium shipments to Peking."

My reply froze on my tongue. If the opium had reached Peking, then it could have found its way into my mother's hands. Or Emperor Yizhu's.

"Are you certain?" I asked, my heart racing. I trusted my mother when she promised she would no longer seek out opium, but someone had procured the drug for the Son of Heaven. And numerous officials and eunuchs still indulged in it, despite all the edicts and decrees.

"There was some effort to make the drug less potent," Yang reasoned. "The samples I isolated had less of the opiate compounds, but the mixture was a stronger hallucinogenic."

Right before I'd fled Yang's ship a year ago, I'd found disturbing evidence down in the cargo hold. "Are you experimenting on people?" I demanded. "Making them sick?"

He was shocked by my accusation. "Those were my men, afflicted after a visit to an opium den in Macau. It was my first clue something was wrong with the opium supply."

Chang-wei and I had witnessed isolated incidents of a strange affliction, seemingly brought on by opium use. Instead of the typical laconic stupor, the afflicted first fell into a comatose state before waking enraged. In Changsha, it had even been mistaken for mad dog sickness.

Was it spreading? And why did we encounter such resistance when we wanted to study opium at the Ministry's laboratory?

"I must warn the Emperor," I said. "And all of Peking."

"It seems you've inherited Chen Chang-wei's blind obedience to his masters," Yang remarked casually.

I threw him a cutting look. "Between your hatred and Chang-wei's sense of righteousness, at least Chang-wei can grow and change. Your hatred can't go anywhere."

Turning on my heel, I reached the door before Yang called to me. "He asked me to watch after you if something were to happen to him."

I looked back. "How could you possibly watch after me when I'm in Peking and you're sailing the oceans as an outcast?"

He grinned. "How did you think I knew to be in Nagasaki at this exact time, *mime*?"

I HAD SEEN the treaty port of Shanghai from the mainland, but to approach by sea was another matter. It was nothing like the guarded bay at Nagasaki, with a few ships dotting the harbor. Western steamships and airships were thick in the sea and air.

How many of the cargo ships out there were transporting crates of opium? Nothing but opium. There was little the trading ships brought that was of any use to us. The foreigners shipped the poison to our shores, and we were forced to let them in. And our populace breathed the black smoke into our lungs, willingly enslaved.

The invasion was already here. The war already lost. And men like Chen Chang-wei worked in secret, quietly waiting for the fight to begin again.

"You can still join with us," Chang-wei said to Yang as we stood on the bow.

Yang's expression was unreadable. "No. I can't."

"It won't remain like this forever."

Together they surveyed the port, taking in the iron monsters. I hadn't mentioned Lord Sagara's secret organization to either of them. I was almost certain they'd laugh at me for being foolish.

"Take care," I told Yang.

"Remember what I told you." His eyes met mine, and I knew what he spoke of. Peking and the tainted opium. We would meet again; I was certain of it.

We said farewell to our companions before disembarking. I was sad to see Satomi go. For a little while, I had imagined she would join me in the imperial city. With her gunsmith skills, we would have found a place for her. But she had preferred to remain alone when she had been in Nagasaki. She and Makoto had left their homeland behind, but they were certainly not ready to pledge loyalty to a new empire.

Chang-wei and I set foot on Chinese soil once again, and I felt both a flood of relief and tension. We were home, but now there was work to do. The familiar smells and sounds of the city hit me as we cleared the docks.

At the trading house, Chang-wei produced a jade seal that proclaimed his rank. "Take me to the Governor General of Ning-po," he commanded.

The lowly clerk looked from the seal to us in confusion before disappearing to seek out a superior. We didn't have the look of important officials in our travel-worn attire.

"It will take some time and an army of bureaucrats," Chang-wei told me. The first signs of weariness were finally showing around his eyes. "But soon we'll be on our way back to Peking."

I WOULD ALWAYS FEEL a sweep of emotion upon returning to Peking. It was the place of my birth, the seat of our empire. A place of palaces and temples.

The first time I had flown over it, my brother Tian was by my side. He had been raised onto his toes, clinging to the rail to peer down into the capital. *Look at that! There's the Summer Palace!* We had pointed out the sights to each other, two excited children, though he was nine and I was eighteen.

"There's the Imperial Academy and the Ministry of Science."
I had pointed out a cluster of structures outside the dome of the
Forbidden City, and we both had fallen silent in reverence. Those
were our sacred temples, where we hoped to worship.

This time there was only Chang-wei and me standing side by
side. A cool breeze blew around us, whipping my hair back as I
closed my eyes and breathed it in. His hand closed over mine.

I opened my eyes to look at him. His focus was down below,
below and inward. There was something so beautiful and distant
in his profile at that moment. As if I had more of a sense of him
than he did. I could almost see his mind working away, ready for
the next task, but his hand was still on mine.

"I wish we could have accomplished more," Chang-wei said
with a sigh.

I know he had hoped for collaboration between our two
empires, but even though we were neighbors, the empire of Japan
and our kingdom were worlds apart. Japan had made a concerted
effort to set itself apart from us, and we had done our part to
sever ties.

"With the American fleet sailing toward Edo, perhaps their
thoughts on an alliance will shift in the future," I said.

"Perhaps," Chang-wei echoed absently. "Perhaps."

But for now, our two nations had their own enemies to face.

23

A n escort was waiting for us at the airfield outside the Summer Palace. We were ushered into a carriage with little ceremony and taken directly to the Forbidden City.

Headman Aguda, clad in his black robe, met us outside the Grand Council. His gaze flickered to me before centering on Chang-wei.

"My report will be ready by tomorrow morning," Chang-wei told him.

"You can give your report directly, Engineer Chen."

Chang-wei frowned at the breach in protocol. It was late in the day—long after the Emperor had halted all audiences.

"You as well, Miss Jin," the head of security said when I stood back. "In case there are any questions."

The Emperor had seemed so dismissive of Chang-wei's proposal, I was surprised there was such interest now. But next to the Emperor, the Grand Council held the highest authority in the land.

Before entering, Chang-wei relinquished a long wooden case to Headman Aguda. It held the Sagara flintlock rifle, beautifully crafted in wood and steel. Aguda opened the barrel and checked for ammunition. When satisfied there was none, he set the firearm back in the case. He didn't hand the case back to Chang-wei. Instead, he held on to it and beckoned with a nod of his head for us to follow.

The chamber was a small, intimate space. Five men were seated around the table with Emperor Yizhu sitting at the head. Membership in the council was by the Emperor's appointment. It could be as few as two and as many as twenty. To the left of Yizhu sat his brother Yixin, titled as Prince Gong, who was the head of the council. The others were all high-ranking Manchurians of noble blood. And then there was Chang-wei and me standing before them.

Emperor Yizhu showed no visible reaction to seeing Chang-wei alive and well, even though the forbidden treatment they'd forced upon him would have killed him by now. It was entirely possible Yizhu had never known. Where had the order come from? Headman Aguda? The Grand Council?

Aguda set the rifle down before the Emperor, opening the case to display the weapon. Emperor Yizhu stared at it, his expression flat. I could tell he was unmoved by the firearm, no matter how sleek and deadly it was. Gunpowder had originated with our engineers, and our cannons had already failed us against the West.

Finally Yizhu nodded dispassionately. "What else?"

Chang-wei knelt and placed the scroll before him. With one sharp tug, the length of silk unfurled like the whip of a dragon's tail.

The scroll stopped dramatically at the foot of the dais where the Grand Council could stare down at it. These weren't the vague sketches and diagrams I had seen in Chang-wei's notebook. What he had compiled to present to the Emperor was something far grander.

It was a vision. A scene that spoke so clearly, Chang-wei didn't need to say a word. A mechanical legion stood shoulder to shoulder from one end of the scroll to the other. Each warrior was outfitted with masks, body armor and weaponry more fearsome than even the *hitokiri* we had faced.

Chang-wei had replicated the same image again and again so his vision was unmistakable. Firepower, steel and numbers. And within each breastplate was a glowing power source, painted as blue fire. That part was his own embellishment, but it presented a dramatic visual.

As the Grand Council surveyed the scroll, Chang-wei reached into his robe and extracted a metallic object. He placed it onto the scroll.

"The most important weapon of all," he announced.

It was the electrical cell. The source of power that had restarted Chang-wei's heart when it stopped beating, but that one surge had burnt it out. Had he repaired it?

He turned the dial, and the cell began to vibrate, humming to life with a loud whir of gears. There was something else. A light began to glow through the glass plate of the device. It shined blue.

This wasn't the same electrical cell Lord Sagara had created. It was something new.

I searched Chang-wei's expression and knew the answer. What one man could do, another could do. He'd lain in bed for the last part of the journey, but he wasn't resting.

"An army," Yizhu murmured, thoroughly enthralled.

"Unlike the world has ever seen, Imperial Majesty."

Chang-wei bowed his head low, but his tone was anything but humble. He was learning how to appeal to an empire's vanity. My own heart pounded as I stared at the war masks on the scroll. Were there meant to be soldiers inside the armored suits? Or were they all intended to be automatons, built solely for the purpose of destruction?

Karakuri warriors in a clockwork army. A war of blood and smoke and sharp metal gears.

The entire council had fallen silent. This time when Yizhu nodded, they all murmured and nodded in kind.

A weight settled on my chest, and it grew heavier with each breath. Part of me knew this is what we needed, but the other half of my soul recalled the cautionary tales my father had taught me. A million souls had poured their blood and sweat into the ground to build our Grand Canal. The bones of laborers were ground into the mortar that held the Great Wall together. I had thought these were merely tales about tyrants of the past, seduced by power, but I was wrong.

I understood what this clockwork army would cost. Factories erected in the provinces, black smoke filling the air, increased labor conscripts. Not just men and women, but children as well.

"You have done well, Engineer Chen." Despite his words, the Emperor did not appear pleased. "These advancements will suit our new course perfectly."

"Forgive this lowly servant for being away from court for so long. What new course does the Son of Heaven speak of?"

"We have stayed quiet for too long. Our enemies take this for weakness." His voice broke. "The rebels have taken Shanghai."

Chang-wei stiffened beside me, and my breath caught. How had the imperial reinforcements fallen so quickly? Yizhu's hard demeanor wavered, and for a moment he was a just young man, only a year older than myself, with an empire on his thin shoulders. Broken and worn to the bone. A moment later, his youth faded away, and he was Emperor once more.

"We are the children of the dragon," he declared with his jaw locked tight. "The greatest empire under Heaven. It is time for us to show our strength."

The Grand Council all nodded in agreement. All except the Emperor's brother, who kept his head bowed.

"No more diplomacy. No more appeasement," Yizhu declared with a curl of his lip. "From this moment on, we are at war."

War.

Our empire wasn't yet ready for this. Emperor Yizhu had always planned to fight back, but not for years. The *Yangguizi* still occupied our ports. Their steamships barricaded our harbors. I glanced at Chang-wei, who kept his expression impassive as he stared ahead.

"First we take back our cities from these filthy rebels," Emperor Yizhu continued, his voice stronger than I'd ever heard it. As if he were addressing the entire empire rather a small, enclosed room of his closest advisers. "Then we drive out the barbarians. And we do not stop. We do not rest until all our enemies have been destroyed."

I LEFT the Forbidden City the same way I had come. Without fanfare, with Chang-wei at my side. Some people were not meant to be celebrated as heroes. Some people preferred it that way.

He reached out to help me into the carriage. My few belongings had been carefully packed into chests. I had found them that way when I'd returned to my room in the Court of Physicians. The linens had been stripped from the bed, the curtains removed.

I had asked for a reassignment, hadn't I? Sometimes petitions within the imperial palace took months to be fulfilled. Sometimes things happened quickly. I wasn't certain this was a good thing.

We sat side by side while the attendants loaded the transport. I held an imperial decree in my hands, folded and sealed with the Emperor's chop. It had been laid across my worktable in the apothecary. Chang-wei had a similar yellow notice laid across his lap. Also unopened.

"The Emperor wants war," Chang-wei said, his tone somber.

I turned the decree around in my hands. The crisp edges pressed into my palm. "The Son of Heaven's will is our will."

"We're not ready."

When was one ever ready for war? "The Emperor seems to have come to his decision quickly," I conceded. "But perhaps a show of strength is not a bad approach."

"This is more than a show of force," Chang-wei said, scowling. "And we have two enemies to fight. The foreigners and the rebel army."

Three. Three enemies, I wanted to say. After what the imperial court had done to Chang-wei, I couldn't trust them anymore. I would continue to follow orders for the sake of unity, but there would be a time we would need to defy imperial command in order to preserve the empire. It was inevitable, and we needed to be prepared.

I leaned forward to slide the beads of the abacus control board to the coordinates for my mother's home. The carriage would go there first before returning to Chang-wei's residence.

As I sat back, the gears and rotors whirred to life, turning the wheels to propel us. The palace gates rolled by with the guardsmen standing aside.

Soon we were in the capital city. The Peking that most people knew of. Rickshaw drivers lounged at the corners, seeking out their next fare. Vendor carts packed the lanes, filling the air with the smell of hot grease and spices.

"So what happens now?" I asked.

He looked down at his yellow envelope. "That depends on what's in here."

Tension knotted my shoulders. I hadn't dared to look at mine yet, and neither had Chang-wei. The two decrees could send us to opposite sides of the empire.

We had returned from Nagasaki to a court already in motion. In the bureaucracy of the imperial palace, everything moved at a snail's pace unless the Emperor asserted his divine right. Yizhu was all but claiming that Heaven wanted this war. Our ancestors wanted this war.

"Together?" I proposed.

Chang-wei held his notice up beside mine. "No matter what it says in here, I meant what I told you Soling. When I think of the future, I see myself with you. Only with you. I don't know what will happen tomorrow or the next day, but we will be together. Some day."

I nodded, my heart in my throat. I couldn't trust myself to say anything at the moment. I hoped what he saw in my eyes was enough.

We broke the seals in unison. For a moment, only the sound of tearing paper filled the carriage. I held my breath as I unfolded the decree.

For a full minute, I did nothing but stare at the contents, assuring myself that the same two characters appeared on both of our assignments. Chang-wei's fingers twined through mine as the carriage rolled on. His touch was warm.

There had been no time to talk about what was to become of us. We hadn't kissed again, either, but every glance and slightest brush had become in some way a kiss. That one precious moment between us, held on to and drawn out. Whatever happened in the days to come, I knew Chang-wei would be there.

It wasn't fate. It was fate that we would make happen.

AUTHOR'S NOTE

Thank you for reading *Clockwork Samurai*, Book 2 of *The Gunpowder Chronicles**. Please consider taking the time to leave a review online. Whether positive or negative, reviews help readers discover new books. I do appreciate each and every review.

These stories are set in the Opium War steampunk world of *The Gunpowder Chronicles*. The first book, *Gunpowder Alchemy*, is set in China and the adventure continues in the second book, *Clockwork Samurai*, which ventures into 19th century Japan.

Tales from the Gunpowder Chronicles, a collection of novellas exploring the secondary characters and subplots of the main series is set to release at the end of 2017. Sign-up for my newsletter to receive updates and freebies: http://bit.ly/contactjeannie

For more information about the series and other books, go to www.jeannielin.com. You can also reach me via the Contact page there. I love hearing from readers!

*The series was originally published in 2014-2015 by InterMix Books.

EXCERPT FROM TALES FROM THE GUNPOWDER CHRONICLES

"The Island"

Note: This excerpt is presented to you prior to final revisions and copy edits. The content may contain differences from the final published copy.

I lived upon a madman's ship, cast away on the endless ocean. For the last month, the aforementioned master of the vessel remained below deck on most days, locked inside his workroom with his experiments. There were parts of the hold that the crew had warned us were forbidden. Trespassing into those nether reaches would lead to abandonment on the nearest shore. And we were under no circumstances to go near the engine room.

These rules did not cause any suspicion or alarm for me. I, Sagara Satomi, daughter of Lord Sagara Shintarō, had grown up surrounded by scientific minds and their peculiarities.

On this particular day, I had brought my firearms above deck to tend to them. The salt air was enemy to the metalwork and I preferred the sunshine to the dim quarters below. Even if the vast ocean surrounding us constantly reminded me that I was far beyond my home, never to return.

Makoto, my fellow countryman, stood nearby. His gaze was fixed out over the water, pointing in the direction of our forsaken country. I knew he looked toward Nippon even though we had drifted far from its shores.

A sense of loss had filled me when the islands had first disappeared into the horizon. The pain had been been sharp and unexpected. I had left Nippon by choice just as Makoto had, but for different reasons.

He'd come searching for a way to reunite with his lost love, a merchant's daughter who had once resided in Nagasaki. As for me—I didn't know what I was searching for. I had merely refused to stay and wait for death as my father had. A samurai would insist that this was cowardice, but my family were samurai no longer.

By law, no one had set foot outside of Nippon was ever allowed to return. If Yang Hanzhu hadn't accepted us onto his ship, we'd have no home.

Today Yang stood at the bow, paging slowly through a tattered book. The ocean breeze rifled the edge of the pages. He took out a spyglass from the pocket of his long-coat and extended it toward the horizon.

In Nagasaki, Yang Hangzhu had a reputation among the tojin in the foreign settlement. Not a Westerner, but certainly not a typical *Shina-jin* either. His coat was fashioned from tanned leather and cut in a rigid-looking shape that extended to his knees. He left it unfastened, revealing a white linen shirt and a row of buttons. Compared to kimono, the clothing was overly complicated. Intricate without purpose.

Whatever he was searching for through the spyglass, it didn't take long. He collapsed the tube and tucked it away, producing a cigarette from his breast pocket in its place. Another one of the oddly Western habits he'd adopted along with his clothing and his hair which had been hacked off at shoulder-length. The significance of such a drastic change was understood even in Nippon. A man who had cut off his queue could never return to Shina.

Yang lit with a some sort of tinder device that closed with a snap. A cloud of smoke billowed around him as he continued to stare at the horizon. I wondered if the habit was a replacement for opium smoke. In Nippon, we considered opium to be a Shina-jin disease and, for all I knew, all of Shina consumed it. We had witnessed how the poison had taken down an entire empire. It was why we forbade the drug from entering our nation.

With a sideways glance Yang started toward us. Bitter smoke wafted toward me, scratching the back of my throat. Yang noticed my reaction and flicked the cigarette aside before closing the distance.

"Sagara-san." His greeting contained all the appropriate words, but far from the proper amount of respect.

"Yang-san."

At Yang's approach, Makoto edged closer. He insisted on acting as my protector though I never asked it of him. I was fallen nobility, but he was fallen samurai. I suppose that meant I still held rank over him. Yang's gaze flicked momentarily to the swordsman before returning his attention to me.

"We will encounter land by tomorrow morning. I would humbly ask that you accompany me when we disembark."

"I would humbly ask for what reason?"

His eyes glinted with amusement. "More to the point, I would ask that your firearms accompany me."

"Can your crewmen not protect you?"

Yang shrugged. "I've seen how you shoot."

I held a bone-handled pistol which I'm certain he had only seen me fire once. We had escaped Nagasaki together, a group of us at once fighting and fleeing assassins sent by the shogunate. I suppose once was all he needed to see. I could aim and my weapons shot straight. I knew some things about Yang Hangzhou as well. He did not show fear in the face of danger, but where ever we were going, he was expecting a good deal of it.

"With respect, I must ask what we will be facing."

The corner of his mouth lifted, not quite a smile. "I wish I knew."

I slid the pistol into its holster and straightened, my gaze hard on him.

"We are headed to an island," he relented. "Off the coast of Guangdong province to the south. We'll approach in the night and dock on the eastern shore opposite the mainland to avoid any patrols."

"Are you smuggling opium?"

Yet met my gaze directly, but didn't answer.

"I know you have opium on this ship." I'd seen a case of it loaded at the last port. The men spoke of visits to opium dens when docking at various ports, though opium smoking was prohibited on board.

"The last thing I would smuggle is opium."

I nodded once. His word was enough. "I am in your debt. I'll go with you."

He grinned and turned to leave, lighting a fresh cigarette and taking a drag before addressing me one last time. "You could have refused, Sagara-san. Honor no longer binds anyone on this ship. There is only free will."

Tales from the Gunpowder Chronicles is set to release December 2017. Sign up for Jeannie Lin's newsletter to receive updates and alerts.

ACKNOWLEDGMENTS

Writing this book was like going to a Vegas buffet where you get to pick and choose all your favorite things and put them all on the same plate: Asiana, history, science, romance, and a whole lot of general geekery. Once again, I have to thank my agent Gail Fortune, who was behind this concept from the moment it was hatched. Thank you to my editors Cindy Hwang and Kristine Swartz for your continued support on and off the page.

As this was my first major foray into a Japanese setting, the Authors of Asian novels group really came through for me. To the AoAN, I can't thank you enough for your inspiration, guidance and support on *Clockwork Samurai* as well as for the teaser short story, "The Warlord and the Nightingale."

To the Doomed Foursome – thank you for all of your support and late night/early morning chats. You keep me going, you really do.

And finally to Dayna Rowan, who once again saved my butt, saved the opening chapters, saved the world – at least my steampunk world: I couldn't have done this without you. I send to you the biggest hug these little arms can manage.

HISTORICAL NOTES ON CLOCKWORK SAMURAI

This was my first work set in Japan which, believe it or not, has very little overlap with my research into Chinese history and culture. Even though this work is a steampunk alternative history, I wanted to ground the culture as much as possible within this time period—the critical moment where these cultures come into collision with Western forces, often against their will.

A large part of my research revolved around how the Chinese and Japanese would interact with one another during this time period, including the not so trivial matter of what they would call each other. For place names and descriptions, I tried to find a balance of historical accuracy and familiarity.

I chose to refer to Japan as "Japan" rather than "Nippon" in the text. The Japanese word for their country is Nippon or Nihon which share the same kanji representation: 日本. This was a very difficult choice for me and I went back and forth several times, but settled on using Japan for familiarity to the Western eye and ear as I was introducing many other elements which might be unfamiliar.

The Japanese characters in the story refer to the Chinese in two ways. "Shina-jin" which technically means "China man" or

"Chinese person", though this term later took on a much more negative and derogatory context, especially during the Sino-Japanese War in the 20th century. The usage of "shinajin" in a contemporary setting would be considered an insult. I made the decision to use this term as during this era, it was still a neutral, descriptive term. The two characters who refer to our protagonist as "Shina-jin" do use it in somewhat of a taunting manner. My selection and usage of the term was meant to embody tension between these two cultures as well as reflect historical context—but it was definitely not meant to be an insult.

The second term, *tôjin*, was also used in Japan during this period to refer to Chinese people. This term is used in the book to refer specifically to the Chinese merchants who traded within Nagasaki.

The story takes place during the Japanese closed country policy, known as *sakoko*. Japanese were not allowed to leave their homeland and foreigners were not allowed to enter except through several controlled access points. All trade was indeed limited to a single trading post in Nagasaki. The Chinese quarters, known as the *tôjin yashiki (Chinamen's mansions)*, was located in a walled off section of Nagasaki. Dutch trade was funneled through the fan-shaped island of Dejima just off the coast. Many of the regulatory details about passage into and out of the trading posts were historically accurate. Prostitutes and entertainers from the mainland were some of the more frequent visitors to Dejima and the *tôjin yashiki*. They were specifically licensed to do so.

The core inspiration for the *Gunpowder Chronicles* series is imagining how steampunk technology would develop in Asia based on the scientific knowledge and culture of China and Japan as opposed to Victorian culture in England. As a result, the popularity of *karakuri* (automatons) in the Edo period played heavily into the formation of my Japanese steampunk aesthetic. *Karakuri* puppets were a novelty and a fad among the wealthy. In *Clock-*

work Samurai, they're first introduced as tea serving puppets as a nod to their actual use as an amusing parlor trick.

The enhanced suits of armor that the assassins used were a nod to mecha suits popularized by *Mobile Suit Gundam* ™ and Veritech fighters in *Robotech*™.

The historical study of science in the West often overlooks contributions from Asian scientists. So much that we have an ongoing myth that the Chinese were advanced in ancient times, inventing gunpowder and the compass (I'm drawing from high school history classes here), but then fell into dark times and isolation and failed to advance. The true story couldn't be farther from that myth. Chinese and Japanese scientists were very well aware of Western developments and were engaged in a vibrant scientific culture that gathered ideas from around the world – even during and despite periods of institutionalized seclusion.

Dutch or Western studies, known as *Rangaku*, were an established field of study among Japanese scientists. The Japanese were interested in Western advancements in physics, chemistry, medicine, and optics. Electrical science was of particular interest. The *elekiteru* (electrostatic generator) featured in the book was a real device developed in Japan.

During my research, I came across scanned pages from some of the *rangaku* texts which were translated into Japanese at the time. Though I was unable to read the text, just looking at the diagrams were both fascinating and educational.

The most fascinating part of my research was reading about the samurai/scientists of the era. The character of Sagara Shintaro, father of Sagara Satomi, is a compilation of several notable scientists of the Edo period, his core inspiration being **Sakuma Shōzan**. Sakuma was a scholar of western studies (*rangaku*) and learned Dutch principles of electricity, which he applied to develop Japan's first telegraph.

I was stricken by the fact that he was assassinated in broad daylight by one of the *hitokiri*, the elite assassins who served the shogunate. Sakuma's biography laid down major pieces of the *Clockwork Samurai* plot in my head.

The character of Takeda Hideyori was based on **Tanaka Hisashige**, also known as Karakuri Giemon which roughly translated means "Automaton wizard". He is often referred to as the Thomas Edison of Japan and founded an organization that eventually evolved into the Toshiba Corporation.

The notable scientists of the time were jack-of-all-trades, many of them working on engineering and creating guns. This is what inspired me to make Satomi a gunsmith. The conflict of the gun vs. the sword is commonly used as a metaphor for traditionalism vs. modernization – I did the same here. Plus the mix of gun and sword-fighting makes for interesting battle scenes.

In truth, there was not as much of aversion to firearms among the samurai class as often assumed. This misconception was probably popularized by Kurosawa films which associated noble samurai with swords and brigands and cowards with firearms. By the sixteenth century, the samurai were using gunpowder and firearms quite effectively in warfare.

Noel Perrin makes the argument that during the Edo Period, Japan did revert back to the sword after a series of arms control measures. (*Giving up the Gun: Japan's Reversion to the Sword*) The work has been disputed by Japanese historians who claim it is more based on the myth of samurai culture than actual fact. Regardless of whether samurai honor culture pushed back on gun usage or favored the sword, by the 19th century and Commodore Perry's famous incursion, Japanese forces were indeed outgunned by the West.

Most likely Japan's isolation policy and also the relative peacefulness of the Edo period made gun warfare less of a necessity.

The American ship mentioned near the end of the story is indeed Commodore Perry's infamous ship, which refused to dock in Nagasaki, but powered on to the capital of Edo to force Japan to end its seclusion policy and open its ports to trade.

ALSO BY JEANNIE LIN

The Gunpowder Chronicles

Gunpowder Alchemy (#1)

Clockwork Samurai (#2)

The Warlord and the Nightingale (short story)

Tales from the Gunpowder Chronicles

The Rebellion Engines (#3)

The Lotus Palace Mystery Series

The Lotus Palace (#1)

The Jade Temptress (#2)

The Liar's Dice (novella) (#2.5)

Harlequin Historicals

Butterfly Swords

The Dragon and the Pearl

My Fair Concubine

The Sword Dancer

A Dance with Danger

Silk, Swords and Surrender (a novella collection)

ABOUT THE AUTHOR

USA TODAY bestselling author Jeannie Lin started writing her first book while working as a high school science teacher in South Central Los Angeles. Her stories are inspired by a mix of historical research and wuxia adventure tales.

Jeannie's groundbreaking historical romances set in Tang Dynasty China have received multiple awards, including the Golden Heart for her debut novel, *Butterfly Swords*. She also writes an Opium War steampunk series and a historical erotica series under the pen name Liliana Lee.

www.jeannielin.com
jeannie@jeannielin.com

35170230R00139

Made in the USA
Middletown, DE
04 February 2019